PENGUIN CLASSICS

THE HOUSING LARK

SAM SELVON (1923–1994) was a Caribbean novelist and short-story writer of East Indian descent, known for his vivid depictions of life in the West Indies and elsewhere. Born in Trinidad, he came to public attention during the 1950s with a number of other Caribbean writers. During World War II, Selvon worked as a wireless operator for the Royal Navy on ships that patrolled the Caribbean, while also writing poetry in his spare time. When the war ended, he went to work at the *Trinidad Guardian*, before eventually moving to London in 1950 and clerking for the Indian Embassy. Soon after, in 1952, he published his first novel, *A Brighter Sun*, followed by eight other novels, among them *I Hear Thunder* (1962), *The Housing Lark* (1965), *Moses Ascending* (1975), and *Moses Migrating* (1983); a collection of short stories titled *Ways of Sunlight* (1958); and a collection of plays titled *Highway in the Sun* (1991). He died in 1994 in Port of Spain.

CARYL PHILLIPS is the author of numerous works of fiction and nonfiction, including *The Lost Child*, *Dancing in the Dark*, *Crossing the River*, and *Colour Me English*. His novel *A Distant Shore* won the Commonwealth Writers' Prize; his other awards include the Martin Luther King Memorial Prize, a Guggenheim Fellowship, and the James Tait Black Memorial Prize. He is a Fellow of the Royal Society of Literature and lives in New York City.

DOHRA AHMAD is Professor of English at St. John's University. She is the author of *Landscapes of Hope: Anti-Colonial Utopianism in America* (2009), coauthor (with Shondel Nero) of *Vernaculars in the Classroom: Paradoxes, Pedagogy, Possibilities* (2014), and editor of *Rotten English: A Literary Anthology* (2007). Her articles have appeared in *ELH*, the *Journal of Commonwealth Literature*, *Pedagogy*, *Social Text*, and the *Yale Journal of Criticism*.

SAM SELVON

The Housing Lark

Foreword by
CARYL PHILLIPS

Introduction by
DOHRA AHMAD

PENGUIN BOOKS

PENGUIN BOOKS

An imprint of Penguin Random House LLC
penguinrandomhouse.com

First published in Great Britain by MacGibbon & Kee, London, 1965
Published in the United States by Lynne Rienner Publishers, Inc., 1990
Published in Penguin Books 2020

LIBRARY OF CONGRESS CATALOGING-IN-PUBLICATION DATA
Names: Selvon, Sam, author.
Title: The housing lark / Sam Selvon ; Foreword by
Caryl Phillips ; Introduction by Dohra Ahmad.
Description: [New York] : Penguin Books, 2020. | Series: Penguin Classics
Identifiers: LCCN 2019040159 | ISBN 9780143133964 (trade paperback) |
ISBN 9780525505747 (ebook)
Subjects: LCSH: Trinidad and Tobago—Fiction.
Classification: LCC PR9272.9.S4 H68.2020 | DDC 813—dc23
LC record available at https://lccn.loc.gov/2019040159

Printed in the United States of America
1 3 5 7 9 10 8 6 4 2

Set in Sabon LT Std

Contents

THE HOUSING LARK

Foreword

The Housing Lark (1965) is a novel that will be immediately recognizable to readers acquainted with Selvon's earlier, and best-known, work, *The Lonely Londoners* (1956). The narrative structure is loose, with various episodes casually strung together, but the "ballads" (or stories) eventually cohere and move toward a poignant conclusion. Selvon peoples his narrative with a motley cast of characters, none of whom we get to know well, but all of whom— as migrants—feel the pressure of living in a new country. They cope with their hurt and alienation by resorting to humor and indulging in outlandish scams. Selvon's thematic concerns are familiar: the pursuit of money, the quest to find work, and the desire to sleep with women. The backbeat to the narrative is an often lyrical meditation on seasonal change as we move from the grimness of winter to the clear blue skies of summer.

The Lonely Londoners is populated with relatively newly arrived migrants—the novel opens with Moses, the main character, catching a bus to Waterloo Station to meet those disembarking from the boat-train—but the characters in *The Housing Lark* are settled in London, and they do not feel it necessary to flaunt their newly acquired knowledge of the streets and bus routes. Brixton is "Brix," but without any fanfare. These Londoners are streetwise enough to know how to hire a coach and an English driver to take them on an excursion to Hampton Court, and they are able to talk about English history (albeit incorrectly) with a sense of proprietorial glee. These are postnostalgia migrants, whose dreams are not populated by thoughts of going home; they have adjusted to both the high and low streets of London and now wish to secure themselves in their new country.

In the 1950s, finding a place to live proved to be a far greater problem for Caribbean migrants than finding a job. Between 1948 and 1962, 250,000 West Indians stepped ashore in Britain to help the Mother Country after the war, but they also wished to take advantage—as British subjects—of the greater opportunities for employment. However, on arriving in Britain, they soon discovered that landlords were disinclined to rent to "colored" people. Signs in windows often read "No Coloureds, No Irish, No dogs." As a consequence, West Indians had little choice but to take inferior rooms in often run-down and unsanitary houses, a situation made worse by the overcrowding that followed as yet more "colored" migrants entered the country. Those who would agree to let to West Indians— most famously the slum landlord Peter Rachman in Notting Hill—charged exorbitant prices while not troubling themselves to maintain their properties.

The rudimentary plot of The Housing Lark concerns itself with the efforts of Battersby—or Bat—a Trinidadian bachelor living in a basement room, to organize a group of his colleagues to club together enough money so that they might put down a deposit on a house and mount the bottom rung of the housing ladder. Such schemes were not uncommon during the fifties and early sixties, but few could have been as hilariously chaotic as that of Bat and

his friends. What they are hoping to achieve is some form
of self-determination and independence from the indigni-
ties visited upon them by being forever overlooked and
ignored in their search for decent housing. What transpires
is something rather different. Among Bat's predominantly
male cohorts there is much double-dealing, and the men
feud and fall out until the West Indian women among them
step forward and take control.

The Housing Lark is a novel that effectively showcases
the central purpose of Selvon's work—the presentation of
the truth, warts and all, of West Indian life transposed to
Britain. He is unsparing in his depiction of the instability
and unreliability of the men who, free from the shackles of
the matriarchal Caribbean, now roam irresponsibly in
patriarchal Britain. He details the feverish search for
women, and the headlong rush to make conquests with
local "birds." In *The Lonely Londoners*, the West Indian
women were marginalized, and even beaten. Not so in this
novel, for it is three West Indian women—Jean, Matilda,
and Teena—who save the day. However, this is certainly
not a feminist novel—women are still grossly objectified,
exploited, and commonly referred to as "the thing"—but
the reality of West Indian survival in Britain, for this early
generation, depended greatly on the resilience and com-
mon sense of the women, and in *The Housing Lark* Selvon
offers more than just a cursory nod of the head in the
direction of this fact.

Selvon's gift was not plot in the conventional sense,
although there is certainly some complexity to his "ballad"
structure, and an eloquence to the manner in which he
juggles his protagonists in and out of the storyline. Also,
deep analysis of character was not Selvon's strength, and
those seeking a full engagement with the psychology of

individuals will be disappointed. However, it would be a
mistake to therefore judge Selvon to be a writer who is simply holding up a sociological mirror in which we might
catch a glimpse of the realities of racial prejudice in Britain
in the austere years between the end of World War II and
the swinging sixties. Selvon was, in fact, a subtle technical
artist who found a form that could best represent the chaotic group life of West Indians in the years when they came
to understand that they had a narrow purchase on life in
Britain, and sadly they could not necessarily rely on each
other—coming as they did from different islands and different traditions. They all had a story to tell, and Selvon
discovered a form in which he might not only give them the
space to tell their individual stories, but also be able to give
them a distinctive voice. Selvon's language is lilting, humor-
ous, and full of compelling imagery, yet always, like the
men themselves, its principal aim is seduction. The insistent
patter of his sentences, their honesty, and the urgency of
their awkward delivery, immediately draws the reader in.
For instance, the opening lines of *The Housing Lark* almost
leap off the page with an accusatory exuberance.

> But is no use dreaming. Is no use lying down there on your
> backside and watching the wallpaper, as if you expect the
> wall to crack open and money come pouring out, a nice
> woman, a house to live in, food cigarettes, rum.

Selvon's great "discovery" was that, unlike the British
"Angry Young Men" of the period—writers such as John
Braine, Alan Sillitoe, and Keith Waterhouse—whose novels are narrated in standard English with the dialogue in
working-class, or northern, dialect, in order to best illus-
trate the realities of West Indian life in Britain he would

have to offer up both narration *and* dialogue in dialect. As
he stated (speaking about *The Lonely Londoners*):

> When I wrote the novel . . . I had in store a number of won-
> derful anecdotes and could put them into focus, but I had
> difficulty starting the novel in straight English. The people I
> wanted to describe were entertaining people indeed, but I
> could not really move. At that stage, I had written the nar-
> rative in English and most of the dialogues in dialect. Then
> I started both narrative and dialogue in dialect and the
> novel just shot along.

Selvon's meticulously observed narratives of displaced
Londoners' lives, using the rich linguistic chords of the
character's voices, created a template for how to write
about migrant, and postmigrant, London for countless
writers who have followed in his wake, including Hanif
Kureishi and Zadie Smith.

Between 1950, when Selvon arrived in England from
Trinidad as a twenty-seven-year-old writer, and 1978,
when he left for Canada, Selvon's ear was attuned to the
pain behind the laughter in the voices of the West Indians
who had left behind their homes and were attempting to
settle in Britain. *The Lonely Londoners* may be his most
famous novel, but *The Housing Lark* is a fine, and unfairly
neglected, companion novel that explores the same thematic material while reaching slightly different conclusions—
particularly so regarding the role of West Indian women.
But in this novel, Selvon, once again, rightly emphasizes
the degree to which the difficulties of migrant life changed
with the four seasons, and he points up the often spiritu-
ally necessary trauma-bonding among small dysfunctional
groups of West Indians, all while drawing our attention to

the individual courage required to simply endure when everything seems to be arrayed against you. Selvon's Londoners are always lonely, but mercifully by the end of *The Housing Lark* they appear to be slightly more organized.

CARYL PHILLIPS

Introduction

On every level, Sam Selvon's *The Housing Lark* is a novel about community. From its unconventional narrative voice, to its ingenious ballad form, to its triumphant plot, to its wry observations about race, nationality, gender, food, music, and history, the novel at once depicts and enacts the coming together of West Indian emigrants in postwar London. *The Housing Lark* may not be Selvon's masterpiece. That honor could belong to *A Brighter Sun*, Selvon's complex Bildungsroman set in rural Trinidad, or *The Lonely Londoners*, his bittersweet exploration of new arrivals to London. However, *The Housing Lark* is a unique and wonderful novel, comic and serious, cynical and tender-hearted, that deserves a wider audience than it has had so far.

Unlike *A Brighter Sun*, *The Lonely Londoners*, and others of his better-known novels, *The Housing Lark* rarely appears in courses on Caribbean, Black British, or postcolonial literature, and is all but absent from a scholarly volume of *Critical Perspectives on Sam Selvon*. Yet it is not for lack of quality that the academic canon has abandoned *The Housing Lark*. Rather, it seems that required reading lists often can't accommodate humor. With its surprisingly happy ending and irreverent, spirited wit, *The Housing Lark* goes against the grain of much postcolonial literature. Typically of vernacular literature, *The Housing Lark* holds its lessons and its literary achievement lightly, offering lessons in history and politics without forcing them on readers. An extraordinarily unified artistic accomplishment, the novel presents a remarkably synthetic vision of West Indian diasporic community and its associated cultural, linguistic, intellectual, and political values.

The Housing Lark shares with *The Lonely Londoners* and Selvon's *Moses* trilogy the topic of West Indian migrant lives in London. In response to a postwar labor shortage, the United Kingdom's government encouraged its Commonwealth citizens to emigrate beginning in 1948. After arriving, the new inhabitants faced white supremacy and xenophobia in multiple forms, including social segregation, housing bias, and employment discrimination. Yet Trinidadians, Jamaicans, Barbadians, Grenadians, Guyanese, and others continued to emigrate until the British government erected legal barriers in 1971. Published in 1965, *The Housing Lark* belongs to a slightly later wave of immigration than the better-known novels of Selvon, George Lamming, V. S. Naipaul, and others; its characters are already somewhat established in London but still figuring out their way. Most significantly, whereas the government predominantly recruited male migrants in the 1950s, more women began to arrive in the following decade. Accordingly, the novel's female characters play a significant role in its plot and themes.

That plot, roughly, involves the "lark" or quixotic idea of buying a home together. Each of the novel's main characters has encountered variations of racist and predatory rental markets, and together they scheme to find a literal and figurative place of their own. From its opening scene, *The Housing Lark* poses the question of whether the lark can become a reality: Will these motley folks, male and female, black and Indian, from Trinidad and Jamaica, prostitutes, housecleaners, factory workers, and hustlers, manage to achieve this milestone of upward mobility? More than any other of Selvon's novels, *The Housing Lark* explores the possibility of unity in difference. Its genius is the way that it expresses that possibility on the multiple levels of form, language, plot, and themes.

*   *   *

The Housing Lark explores the quest among migrants for a place to be fully human. Before we think about how that topic manifests itself on the more obvious levels of plot and themes, it's important to begin by thinking about *how* the novel conveys its central interests. Rather than a conventional chapter structure, Selvon has chosen to shape his novel according to "ballads," or character-based episodes. Though carefully thought out and brilliantly executed, this unusual structure has the effect of appearing spontaneous and unmediated. Our impression is of a friend associatively recounting stories; the novel, in fact, is perfectly assembled to make the points and create the effect that Selvon intends.

As the Barbadian poet and literary theorist Kamau Brathwaite writes in his critical study *History of the Voice*, calypso has often provided a central format and aesthetic for West Indian writing. Whereas Brathwaite's topic is poetry, in *The Housing Lark* calypso influences the shape of the work of art on the most macro levels of plot and novelistic form as well as at the more line-by-line level of rhythm and language. To my mind, *The Housing Lark* represents one of fiction's most fortuitous marriages of form and content: every character's fate is linked to that of others; they form a community together; and that interdependence comes across perfectly in the overall shape of the novel. Whenever we move from one character to the next, the anonymous narrator navigates the novel's terrain in a

very careful, deliberate way: out to a new ballad, then back
in again to the main storyline, the search for a place that
these individuals, together, can call their own. Thoroughly
in control of the narrative, Selvon's narrator masterfully
balances individual and communal stories.

Selvon employs an extraordinarily innovative narrative
voice, which I would call "embodied omniscient." Like a
traditional omniscient narrator, this one has no name or
specific persona, and is aware of the inner thoughts and
motivations of all the characters. Yet he also identifies himself as part of their community, an individual with raced,
nationalized, gendered characteristics. He is clearly male,
of West Indian origin, a fellow migrant. At once mocking
and sympathetic, he is immersed in the lives of his characters, respects their linguistic choices, and follows the main
character Battersby's cues to label him "Bat" and his mod-
est apartment "number 13a" according to Bat's preference.

Anglophone vernacular fiction, i.e., fiction in any non-
standard variety of English, tends to fall into two catego-
ries: either an omniscient narrator uses Standard English,
while characters speak in vernacular (as in Zora Neale
Hurston's *Their Eyes Were Watching God* or Roddy
Doyle's Barrytown Trilogy), or there is a vernacular-
speaking first-person narrator (as in Mark Twain's *Huck-
leberry Finn*, Sapphire's *Push*, Ken Saro-Wiwa's *Sozaboy*,
and many others). Selvon's novels are extremely rare in
their choice to bestow *narrative authority*—in other words,
objective knowledge—on a vernacular narrator. Perhaps
only Earl Lovelace (in *The Wine of Astonishment* and
other fiction) and Oonya Kempadoo (in *Tide Running*)
have also created omniscient vernacular narrators, and
those came decades after Selvon's innovation.

Even beyond the innovative choice of omniscient vernacular narrator, this is a novel in love with West Indian

Vernacular English (WIVE). Like the novel's form and narrator, its linguistic medium, too, works to create and reinforce a sense of community and belonging. Consider the following ode to Selvon's subject and method:

> If you ever want to hear old-talk no other time better than one like this when men belly full, four crates of beer and eight bottle of rum finish, and a summer sun blazing in the sky. Out of the blue, old-talk does start up. You couldn't, or shouldn't, differentiate between the voices, because men only talking, throwing in a few words here, butting in there, making a comment, arguing a point, stating a view. Nobody care who listen or who talk. Is as if a fire going, and everybody throwing in a piece of fuel now and then to keep it going. It don't matter what you throw in, as long as the fire keep going—wood, coal, peat, horse-shit, kerosene, gasoline, the lot. (99)

Selvon draws a compelling parallel among language, community, and his own novel: talk is life, life is literature, literature is talk. WIVE, here, functions as both a metaphor and a medium for the idea of communal endeavors and survival in the colonial metropolis. This is the essence of Selvon's undertaking and his success.

In an equally concrete tribute to his chosen language, Selvon includes explanations of some terms with which a non–West Indian reader would be unfamiliar. This is a quintessential technique of vernacular literature, which often self-consciously builds the literacy of its audience. After using the word "buttards," the narrator parenthetically but proudly declares "(That's a good word, but you won't find it in the dictionary. It mean like if you out of a game, for instance, and you want to come in, you have to buttards, that is, you pay a small fee and if the other players agree, they allow you to join. It ain't have no word in the English language to mean that, so OUR PEOPLE make it up)" (92). Internal gloss, or a definition encapsulated within a literary work, appears frequently within vernacular fiction; here, it is fitting that the novel's most prominent internal gloss involves the topic of community and belonging. Just as "OUR PEOPLE" invent the word "buttards," so Selvon supplements the English literary canon by offering his own immigrant-centric (in terms of both language and content) contribution.

This is not to say that WIVE is the only language that appears in *The Housing Lark*. Selvon's narrator is a virtuoso of code-switching who employs whichever communicative medium best suits his purposes at a given moment. He often wryly approaches Standard British English from the outside, at once displaying his mastery of it and also pointing out its shortcomings in terms of communication or truth value. The English literary references are vast, from Kipling's "The Ballad of East and West" and Dickens's *Tale of Two Cities* to a radical recontextualization of Biblical verse into a comment on girl-watching ("You could say what you like about the old Brit'n, but when summer come he that have eyes to see let him see" [70].) The novel weaves in the language of journalism, Romantic poetry, weather forecasting, and even math, as the narrator describes the tragicomic side character Syl asking Bat "'So what you think, so what you think,' like a recurring decimal" (77). Though Selvon's deepest love may be for WIVE, it is hard to imagine any way of speaking (i.e., discourse) or of knowing (i.e., epistemology) that he would not use as artistic fodder.

*　*　*

Having outlined Selvon's major achievements in *The Housing Lark* in the areas of form, narrator, and language, I will bring us into this superbly crafted novel at the most logical point: the beginning. The novel's first sentence beautifully encapsulates the important topics and strategies to come. "But is no use dreaming," the narrator boldly begins (1). This *in medias res* opening asserts the validity of the vernacular English that is among the many codes accessible to the narrator, while also setting up the dialectic of "use" (in other words, utility, pragmatism, realism) versus "dreaming" (in other words, fantasy, idealism, romance). The theme of dreams runs through the novel, from the initial and recurring image of genie wallpaper, to the motley cast of absurd dreamers, to the governing dream of a home. Every character has a dream, some more reasonable and plausible than others: Harry Banjo seeks a recording contract; Gallows carries out an "everlasting quest" for a missing five-pound note; Alfy quixotically hopes for instant success as a photographer; Syl chases women across London.

In the poignant passage below, Selvon recognizes the universality and transformative power of dreams:

Is a funny thing, but men have a lot of thoughts and ideas what sleeping inside and never get a chance to come out. If for instance you notice a fellar who quiet and easy with a job that bringing him in about ten quid a week, you put a hundred pounds in his hand and you will see a different man. You might look at this fellar and say he ain't have no ambition, he look so satisfy with this ten quid a week. And bam! you put this hundred quid in his hand, and all them thoughts and ideas what was sleeping yawn and come wide awake. Suddenly this same fellar realise he want a car, or a yacht, or a platinum blonde. Mark you, is not the money what create these ideas: he had them all the time, but only now they getting a chance to breathe. (34–35)

Reconciling the apparent opposites of "use" and "dreaming" that he introduced at the outset, Selvon suggests that dreams, when allowed, will take on their own reality. To survive and build community in a hostile land may take the intervention of a genie, but it can be done. The "lark" of the title, Selvon insists, is at once amusing and deadly serious. While mocking unrealistic dreaming, the novel also valorizes it as a potentially transformative activity— as long as it's combined with some degree of pragmatism. Being unrealistic is the only way that anything will ever change. To return to the beautifully succinct opening "Is no use dreaming," we need "use" (utility or realism) plus "dreaming" (fantasy) in order to effect social change.

As Selvon valorizes both dreaming and realism on the level of plot, so he vacillates between realist and fantastical modes in his narration. "Now, that is exactly how everything happen," his narrator insists at a pivotal moment in the evolution of the central goal.

> If I was writing a story I could make up all sorts of things, that Bat say so-and-so and Jean say this-and-that and Harry say but-what-about.
>
> Because you know how the idea catch on? Just like that? Is so things happen in life. Some words here, a little meeting there, and next thing you know, War Declare, or a Man Gone to the Moon.
>
> And being as I want to tell the truth, I have to say that that is how it happen. (14)

Here we have a realist mission statement: with "is so things happen in life," Selvon uses the conventions of literary realism to justify his central metaphor and its satisfying outcome, which ironically represents a departure from an expected realist ending. This is not overt magic in an English fairy tale mode, but instead a light-handed intervention on the narrator's part, an updated *deus ex machina* in an unexpected guise.

Achieving the dream of a home necessitates the perfect recipe of realism and fantasy; it also necessitates specific contributions from the novel's male and female characters, each of whom Selvon associates with a different approach to the idea of dreams. Jean and Teena, burned before, mistrust the act of dreaming; Matilda offers a breakthrough idea that helps make the "lark" a reality; and it is Teena's pragmatism that resuscitates the plan. When Harry assures Jean, "We will have our own place to live," here is her reply: "'That is only a lark,' Jean say, 'you think them fellars really serious? . . . Everything is 'if.' If this and if that. You fellars does live in a dream world'" (57). For now, Jean provisionally doubts and invalidates the lark of the title; yet, through her, Matilda's, and Teena's assertive interventions, the dream world of the fellars becomes a place that all can inhabit together. Cross-gender cooperation, some unlucky-seeming luck, and strategic appropriation of existing racist stereotypes all mix together to provide a surprise happy ending.

The transformative role of women in *The Housing Lark* represents a departure from Selvon's earlier novels of migration. As Selvon explained in a 1994 interview, "In *The Lonely Londoners*, for instance, there were no women characters but you've got to remember that the time I am writing about, this is when the men went to England before, to look for jobs, and to settle down before they sent for their women and their families to come and join them, so there weren't very many women about then. So to write about later on, like in *The Housing Lark* as I say, they come into play, and I have written about them." Indeed, women come into play not only as characters but as important actors in the novel's central quest.

That is one of the many ways in which *The Housing Lark* challenges a prevailing misogyny that it may sometimes appear to endorse. The male characters (along with the narrator) consistently refer to women as "things"—literally objectifying them, or making them into objects—as well as assuming that they will be responsible for all domestic duties. At the same time, though, the narrator reveals those beliefs as absurd, while also compassionately representing Jean's, Matilda's, and Teena's points of view. The more misogynistic men of *The Housing Lark* come in for gentle, indirect mocking on the part of the narrator—or, rather, the narrator gives them just enough rope to hang themselves. Fitz, for example, boasts that "I am a professor of womanology, boy. If I had five little fingers, I could wrap them around all of them" (30). This is the same Fitz who proves to be an obedient husband to the admirably organized Teena. Anticipating feminist critiques that would emerge several decades later, the novel both illustrates and undermines the language of male supremacy. *The Housing Lark* also roundly depicts a range of female characters' perspectives, including a nonjudgmental and nonromanticized portrait of Jean's experience as a prostitute. As the narrator explains, "To tell you the truth, though Jean was a nice girl, she was a hustler, going up to Hyde Park every evening to look for fares" (12). He later adds, on a counter-discursive note, "Hustling for fares wasn't as easy as people think" (48). Moralizing, Selvon later shows through an amusing episode with some interfering white nuns, is an entirely pointless undertaking.

Again anticipating twenty-first-century gender theory, *The Housing Lark* also illustrates the complex intersections of race and gender. The narrator disavows the English stereotype that "the boys only after white things" (12) as well as illustrating the men's different expectations for relationships with white and West Indian women. We also see how, within that racialized milieu, a character like Syl finds the need to perform a falsely exoticized identity in order to get the interest of white English women. Despite its light, entertaining tone, *The Housing Lark* never simplifies or sugarcoats the complex race and gender dynamics that it depicts.

All of the above—literary form, narrator, language, plot, and the themes of dreaming and gender—factor into a simultaneous portrait and enactment of community. The novel acknowledges the complexity and multiplicity of Caribbean diasporic identities, working to disaggregate any monolithic understanding of what it is to be West Indian. As well as gender, other possible fissures are those of race and nation. In an early scene, the novel portrays Caribbean London as fractured, and the concept of solidarity as self-serving and limited. It is the unsavory, assimilationist rent collector Charlie Victor who first floats the idea of solidarity, cynically encouraging Trinidadian Bat to take a Jamaican roommate—in the guise of regional fellowship, but in reality so that Charlie can collect more rent. Elsewhere, characters of African descent mock the Indo-Trinidadian Syl's shifting identity. However, the action of the novel works to repair those provisional schisms, *enacting* solidarity by creating a pan–West Indian community despite apparent fractures. Solidarity grows by necessity, but ultimately for the benefit of all.

The Housing Lark is about West Indian individuals— dreamers, hustlers, artists—coming together despite the factors of nation, race, and gender that threaten to divide them. Even while insisting on a variety of migrant experience, Selvon also shows how different people converge to create and sustain an art, culture, and politics that ensure the survival of all. Thus the recurrent capitalized phrase OUR PEOPLE, which embodies the expansive but concrete pan-Caribbean grouping that is formed through language. Whereas "in truth and in fact, loneliness does bust these fellars arse" (88), Selvon's novel both embodies and remedies that profound loneliness. The fellars may not return home, but they will get their house.

*   *   *

The Housing Lark celebrates West Indian vernacular cultures in all their multiple manifestations, from language to food, music, religion, nicknames, history, and ultimately to vernacular forms of knowledge. To take the concrete example of food, the novel initially gestures toward bestowing value on "them dishes you does only read about in magazines, chicken a la this and that, T-bone and Z-bone steaks" (2). Later, though, it stakes a claim against a bland, assimilationist diet, drawing a clear contrast between "mash potato and watery cabbage and some thin slice of meat what you could see through" (88) and "all kind of big iron pot with pilau and pigfoot and dumpling, to mention a few delicacies" (84). The loving detail paid to West Indian food points to the need for true nourishment in a foreign and often inhospitable environment.

Music is an equally strong source of pride and community. Formally, calypso gives the novel its ballad shape; calypso also provides the *deus ex machina* happy ending. The charming and optimistic Harry Banjo is a perfect metatextual figure for the artist (whether musical or literary) who brings people together and interprets migrant culture to a broader audience. Like Langston Hughes's ode to internal migration, "Po' Boy Blues," Harry's music merges a pre-existing musical form with reinvented migrant content. Channeling Harry's diplomatically phrased publicity materials, the narrator tells us that "he would be cutting his first disc soon, with some numbers that he compose while awaiting Her Majesty's pleasure in the Brixton jail" (123). Migration and unjust incarceration have changed Harry's music; the pre-existing genre of calypso is made new for a new place and a newly diversified audience. Art, in Selvon's view, is always reinventing itself, for the good of all its consumers. Like *The Housing Lark*, Harry's album is a faithfully West Indian artistic product that could only have existed in diaspora.

Vernacular religious practices make a brief appearance as well. In his ballad on the open-hearted Matilda, Selvon's narrator explains that "Matilda come from a religious family. The religion ain't have no name" (47). This is a perfectly succinct description of a vernacular way of life: here, as in Selvon's observations on food and music, vernacular is not only a linguistic mode but also a way of thinking and being. Along with food, music, and religion, nicknames too signify a vernacular outlook. The nicknames that abound in *The Housing Lark* constitute an insider's shorthand that defines and delineates a community. Nearly every male character has a nickname; the narrator displays his careful negotiation of multiple codes and audiences by establishing their "official" names (Battersby, Fitzwilliams, and so on) and then quickly switching to the more intimate and personal nicknames.

Finally, in the same way that he deflates standard English language, Selvon's narrator also punctures "official" English history. When the characters visit Hampton Court, Henry VIII's sixteenth-century palace, the narrator observes, "You could imagine the old Henry standing up there by the window in the morning scratching his belly and looking out, after a night at the banqueting board and a tussle in bed with some fair English damsel. You could imagine the old bastard watching his chicks as they stroll about the gardens, studying which one to behead and which one to make a stroke with" (94). This moment, among others, displays Selvon's revisionist agenda: to tell the story of West Indian immigration to England from a West Indian point of view. We see competing versions of history, "official" and popular, dominant and subaltern. As Fitz narrates his version of English history to Teena and their children, they're shushed by a disapproving guard: "'Here here, what's all this?' a attendant come up. 'You can't be shouting like that. Move along now'" (95). White supremacist authorities will always be present, telling the immigrants that they don't belong and have no right to interpret the meaning of England. Yet *The Housing Lark* itself defies those authorities, moving along with its characters rather than pushing them away.

Despite its light tone, *The Housing Lark* conveys a complex and crucial debate about education and historiography: Whose history will be told, and how? Later in the same Hampton Court scene, unnamed characters ponder how history will be taught now that West Indian children have entered the English school system in large numbers. The following unattributed dialogue may be spontaneous and conversational, but it contains important and enduring questions about curriculum and national identity:

'I must say you boys surprise me with your historical knowledge. It's a bit mixed up, I think, but it's English history.'

'We don't know any other kind. That's all they used to teach we in school.'

'That's because OUR PEOPLE ain't have no history. But what I wonder is, when we have, you think they going to learn the children that in the English schools?'

'Who say we ain't have history?' (100–101)

The Housing Lark enters this lively, vital, and prescient debate, presenting Selvon's version of Anglo-Caribbean history in the making. The narrator concludes the passage about Henry VIII, "And suppose old Henry was still alive and he look out the window and see all these swarthy characters walking about in his gardens!" (95). As the most xenophobic white English citizens feared, and as Louise Bennett triumphantly predicted in her 1966 poem "Colonisation in Reverse," the presence of West Indian migrants would fundamentally and irrevocably change English culture.

Throughout the novel, the savvy narrator manages to negotiate multiple audiences. Ostensibly, he directs his storytelling to an ignorant, possibly hostile audience of outsiders, those who would tell our characters to "move along now." He alerts that audience that "to introduce you to all these characters would take you into different worlds, don't mind all of them is the same colour!" (15). The novel, the narrator is signaling, will provide both education and literary tourism; and this sector of his audience is in particular need of the educational function. Thus the narrator makes it his mission to disaggregate or break up any outsider's simplistic, monolithic understanding of West Indian identity. He later writes, "To go into more detail—tell you where he come from originally, whether he six foot tall or five foot six, whether he have big eyes and a small nose—what difference it make to you? All you interested in is that he black—to English people, every black man look the same" (15). Over the course of the novel, Selvon's narrator educates that initially ignorant and closed-minded audience by pausing to define vernacular terms like "buttards" and "landan-tweet-tweet-tweet, a game children does play in the West Indies where they have to find something that hide" (41). By the end, he can trust that "I shouldn't have to tell you" a particular detail he now has faith that we will anticipate (87).

While entertaining and diverting, the novel has an explicitly counter-discursive function: Selvon intends it to provide evidence against all the stereotypes and assumptions his characters face in the unwelcoming metropolis. To give one example out of many, "You see, though the newspaper and the radio tell you that people in the West Indies desperate for jobs and that is why they come to Britain, you mustn't believe that that is the case with all of them. I mean, some fellars just pick themselves up and come with the spirit of adventure, expecting the worst but hoping for the best. Some others just bored and decide to come and see what the old Brit'n look like" (56). Fiction, in Selvon's hands, offers an alternative to mainstream media portrayals of immigrants.

At the same time as providing a valuable corrective for its white audience, the novel is also beautifully pitched to West Indian diasporic readers. The unapologetically capitalized phrase OUR PEOPLE appears throughout, often in moments of pride. For both audiences, the novel has a continually defamiliarizing function: in other words, it presents mainstream Anglo culture through the eyes of those who don't take it for granted and therefore can highlight its absurdity and arbitrariness. For example, a brilliant early passage mocks English folk beliefs about the weather: "I mean, you think it have a lot of obeah and black magic in the West Indies, but if you listen to some of these Nordics. They say red sky is shepherd's delight, and if the dog fall asleep that mean rain coming, and if the cat start to play frisk that mean sunshine" (3). As in the scenes at Hampton Court, here we have what we could call a West Indian vernacular epistemology: a form of knowledge that lightly but deliberately challenges Anglocentric ways of thinking.

In this instance, Selvon's narrator deploys humor to deauthorize English forms of knowledge. This is only one of many tactical uses of humor throughout *The Housing Lark*. Indeed, it is a seriously funny novel, in the sense that its wit is both constant and satisfying, and also always in service to important political observations. Selvon's narrator sums up this technique in one of his formal explanations: "Now, I will have to digress with a ballad about Syl, which will help to explain why Syl ain't laughing" (19). Syl ain't laughing about the idea of co-owning a house because he has found his low-status regional identity as a Caribbean migrant at odds with his higher-status racialized appearance as a person of Indian origin. His only way around prejudiced landlords is a desperate masquerade. Syl's "ballad" is at once a profound—and profoundly sad—exploration of the complexities of racial and cultural identity and also a genuinely amusing episode.

The Housing Lark also contains humor that challenges respectability politics and sometimes reproduces English stereotypes of Anglo-Caribbeans. The novel acknowledges the difficulties of being a minority, especially for this group that was accustomed to being a majority in their home islands. Within an overwhelmingly racist structure, as Selvon demonstrates throughout the novel, no individual of color can be seen as an individual; instead, all come to represent their race and nation. Given that condition of hypervisibility, notions of appearance and propriety have a strong implication for literary art, as they lead to the question of which stories should be told, and how. With his staunch commitment to humor and vernacular values, Selvon stakes out a claim against respectability. Rather than participate in the literature of uplift, he is determined to paint a picture of the West Indian immigrant community that is comic and often unflattering, including misogyny, fractures of solidarity, and much generally ridiculous behavior. In keeping with its continuous dual audience, its jokes come at the expense of West Indian as well as English readers. We all are left with the feeling that Teena's accusation "You all can't even get serious" (117) applies at once to Selvon's male characters and also to his novel: in Teena's voice, he indirectly condemns his own methods of comedy and digression. Selvon resists getting too serious, but by the end of the novel shows that he takes Teena's emphasis on pride, appearance, and upward mobility quite seriously. Opposing the literature of respectability and uplift, Selvon asserts that his characters' stories need to be told.

* * *

Much of *The Housing Lark* seems to imply—especially through the voices of its female characters—that dreaming is a self-involved, counterproductive occupation. But by its close the novel takes a radically different and unexpected turn, to valorize the utility of dreaming. A novel that we might have located squarely in the tradition of social realism, with a good dose of parody and caricature thrown in, turns out to participate in a totally different genre of wish-fulfillment. It would be a mistake to read *The Housing Lark* as solely a comic novel, when in fact it carries out a radical act of claiming space and humanity. Just as Selvon shows Harry Banjo's art evolving in a new context, and becoming a hybrid art, Selvon's art as well turns out to be a surprising hybrid of genres. Funny, serious, innovative, multilingual, musical, *The Housing Lark* shows how literary expression can create community and belonging across race, gender, place, and time.

DOHRA AHMAD

The Housing Lark

But is no use dreaming. Is no use lying down there on your backside and watching the wallpaper, as if you expect the wall to crack open and money come pouring out, a nice woman, a house to live in, food, cigarettes, rum. And sometimes in this fantasy he used to rub the wall, remembering Aladdin and the wonderful lamp, just to see if a geni wouldn't come and ask him: 'What you want, just tell me what you want, no matter what it is, I could get it for you.'

The irony of it was that the wallpaper really had a design with lamps on it, Aladdin lamps all over the room. It may be that the company know they could only get dreamers to live in a dilapidated room like that, and they put up this wallpaper to keep the fires of hope burning.

Battersby thought maybe he wasn't rubbing the right one. Suppose, just suppose, that one day he start to rub all of them, looking for the right one. And suppose, just suppose, that say, as he reach that one up in the corner near the ceiling, he rub a geni into life for true!

'What you want, Battersby, you is my master, and anything in the world you want I could get for you.'

'I want money.'

Bam! Pound notes and fivers start to fall all about in the room, until is as if he swimming in it, and the water-mark rising higher and higher!

'I want food.'

All about, on the chair, on the bed, on the mantlepiece, on the ground, dishes start to appear. I mean, though Battersby would of preferred a good dumpling and pigtail, this geni bring them dishes you does only read about in magazines, chicken a la this and that, T-bone and Z-bone steaks, shark fin and bird nest soup, and a little pig roast brown with a apple stick in his mouth, to mention only a few of the things the geni bring, because Battersby don't know the names of any of them.

'I want rum.'

Hmm. The kind of drinks what the geni bring is only for connisears. Red liquers, blue liquers, brandies of all descriptions, wines from the vines of France and Spain, rum from Haiti and Cuba, hock and ale from Cornwall, palm wines from Africa.

'I want a nice woman—I mean, the nicest woman in the world!'

This time the geni take a little longer to produce. And when she come, is as if she float out of a pink mist. The geni say, 'Master, it ain't have no one woman who is the nicest, but this one could change into anything you want. All you have to do is press the right tit, and she would change into whatever you feel for in your mind. If you feel like a stalwart blond from one of the Scandinavian countries, she will turn into one. If you feel like a slim brunette, just press the right tit.'

But is no use dreaming. Battersby, lying down on the bed jam against the corner in this basement room in Brixton, turn over and close his eyes, as if, when he awake, life was a dream, and if he could go back to sleep, everything would be real in the land of nod.

Was the alarm clock what wake him. That is to say, it didn't alarm, because he didn't have to go to work today.

But he so accustom to jumping up five o'clock every morning, that he could never sleep late, even on a Sunday. He push his hand under the bed and haul out cigarettes and lighter. As he light up he wonder what London was like outside. Funny thing in this country, you could never tell what sort of day waiting to pounce on you. It might be raining, sleeting, snowing, shining, bright, dull—you could never tell. With the curtains drawn, is as if another world out there. Sometimes Battersby uses to speculate, like, Sun shining today, and go and pull the curtain to see. When he first come to Londontown, he uses to listen to the weather forecast on the radio. The radio was transi, by the side of the bed, he pay four pound ten for it second hand from the market, it only picking up the Light, the Home, and Luxembourg. But it didn't take long for Bat to realise that when it come to weather forecasting, them fellars don't know their arse from their elbow. When Spring come, is all kind of wild speculation what kind of Summer we going to have. People who have rheumatism and corns on their big toe start up to forecast rain here, thunder there, lightning on the East Coast, hail in Scotland, gales in the Hybrides. I mean, you think it have a lot of obeah and black magic in the West Indies, but if you listen to some of these Nordics. They say red sky is shepherd's delight, and if the dog fall asleep that mean rain coming, and if the cat start to play frisk that mean sunshine. One test write in the newspapers that he does have a tingling in his head during the last week of Spring, and that mean a good Summer coming up. One woman say she doesn't go anywhere unless she consult Flossie. If Flossie bark and want to go out, that mean no rain going to fall. But if Flossie slinking in the corner or sit down scratching fleas, bad weather in the offing.

Some of them so bold-face they not content with a day's

forecast, but want to divine the whole Summer for you,
and on top of that, dividing up the days and weeks, saying
which will be the sunny ones, and to crown it all even telling you what part of the country will get the most sun.
Like if is some great event, newspapers have places all over
the world, and day after day they putting down how long the
sunshine in Saskatchewan, and Constantinople, and the
Isle of Man. Then in the next column, they totting up how
much sun shine in all the days of the Summer so far, as if
the place that had the most sun going to win a prize. Some
of them have some kind of scientific diagrams, with lines
and circles and figures, and to tell you the truth I don't
know anybody who know what all them maps mean, and
perhaps that is a good thing. But the greatest is that on
the TV, they have this big map spread out, and a fellar
come with a stick like a schoolmaster. But this man, who-
ever he is, must be really God, because he only picking up
some clouds and putting it over London and saying, 'Rain
going to fall there tomorrow.' He picking up a laughing
sun and putting it on the West Coast and saying, 'Sun
going to shine there tomorrow.' And he handing you some
smart talk about depressions and areas of high pressure.

The first time Battersby see this fellar on TV—home by
Alfonso, because he ain't have a TV himself—he say to
Alfonso, 'But this man is a giant! You hear how he talking
about depression and high pressure? I mean, them is things
the boys know about!'

And as for the official forecasts, they always handing
you some smart line, like 'Showers, mainly cloudy, sunny
intervals, bright periods.' You don't know if it going to
rain or shine or snow or fog. That is smartness for you,
them fellars should be diplomats. But the beauty of it all is
when you see they feeling cocksure, like when is August
Bank Holiday. And they say, 'It going to be sunny and

warm.' Up in the atmosphere thunder roll with laughter, lightning split its sides laughing, and them clouds laugh so much they cry! And the old wind make a sally across Iceland before coming to Brit'n and bam! August Bank Holiday you get up and you don't know what to do, if to wear jeans, if to wear pullover, if to carry a mack, if to sport a brolly.

And the clamour! People writing all kinds of letters to the Press about the weather. Some blaming the atom bomb, some saying is because the world so evil these days, some suggesting to put up glass roofs on the beaches, so you won't get wet unless you go in the sea.

All them weather forecasters, official and unofficial, they should line them up and shoot them. Battersby himself reach a stage where it don't matter at all—he always expecting the worse, like the basement door can't open because snow pile up against it, or it fogging so much that he can't see to walk up the steps. It had many a time when Bat go out in shirt and trousers and had to rush back down to don pullover and sweater and pullover and merino and sweater and mack. In fact, as this is no continuous ballad, I might as well take the opportunity of telling you about the Summer day that Bat went out, in corduroy trousers and jitterbug shirt. I mean, if you can't take a chance in the Summer, when you going to take it, pray? The sun was shining, the sky was blue. He was meeting a thing by Notting Hill Gate. He was all right in the underground, but when he surfaced at the station, as if in that hour time the sun change its mind, and the sky haul out some grey blankets. By the time he and the thing reach out on the pavement, Bat shivering like an aspen leaf.

'Why didn't you put on more clothes?' the thing ask him. These Englishers don't take them dangerous chances—she herself well muffle up and have on a coat.

'The weather was looking all right,' Bat say. Then he say, 'Wait here for me,' and he dash into a second hand clothes shop. Bat emerge with a thick trousers and a coat, and he went down in the Gents and come back up, ready to face the elements.

Well, Bat went and pull the basement curtains to peep out. It look all right for the time being. He went by the gas ring near the mantlepiece and put on the kettle to make a cup of tea. He smoke another cigarette while the kettle boiling. He was thinking about ways and means of making money. This is a perpetual thought with the boys, but Bat was at a stage when things was getting desperate. Funds was running so low that he couldn't manage. Three pound ten rent for the basement, for one thing, and he only had three pound left out of his wages. But being as it was Sunday, he felt sure that somebody bound to drop around to see him, and he would borrow a couple of quid. Funny thing, when you put it that way, it don't sound like money at all. I mean, if you ask somebody to lend you two pounds, they might hem and haw, but if you go up to them and say, 'Lend me a couple of quid, boy, I broken,' then it sound as if you were only asking them to scratch your back, or to light your cigarette or something.

And Bat had a way, he used to be so cool and casual that before you know it he tap you for a quid. 'I don't think of money at all,' Bat used to tell the boys. 'I mean, what is money? It only get you in a lot of trouble—' and right here he splice in with 'see if you have any change in your pocket and lend me ten bob,'—and carrying on with the topic as if there wasn't any interruption—'yes, I know a Jamaican what was saving up money. He save about seven hundred quid, and one day he was crossing the road by Marble Arch and a car knock him down and he dead. He dead right there, and they find this seven hundred lock up in a suitcase under the bed, and take it for Death Duty.'

Very often, Bat catch fellars like that, until one day Fitz-williams decide to put a stop to it. As Bat start up to sing about the evils and uselessness of wealth, Fitz only nodding agreement. When Bat splice in the request for a loan in midstream, Fitz pretend he ain't hear. After a minute Bat make another splice in the conversation, and still Fitz ain't hear. Fitz in the meantime carrying on even stronger than Bat on the topic, nodding vigorously, elaborating a point, making references, drawing analogies, until suddenly Bat stop.

'How much you want?' Bat ask him.

'Ten bob,' Fitz say.

'Here,' Bat say, and give him the money.

All the same, a sucker is born every day, and though Fitz turn the tables on Battersby, it had about three hundred thousand other infants who would fall for his spiel.

Battersby open up a tin of Brunswick sardines and put them in a plate. He slice up a onion and two tomatoes, and mix it up with the sardines. He put in some olive oil and some pepper sauce, and mash up everything until it come like a paste. He sweeten his tea with condensed milk, and then sit down on the one chair by the table, and begin to eat breakfast.

He hardly put the first bite in his mouth before the basement door knock.

'Who the arse is that so early?' Bat say to himself, because it wasn't even seven o'clock yet. He went by the window and draw the curtain a little and peep out.

He see Charlie Victor stand up there. He drop the curtain and tip-toe back to the table. Charlie Victor come to collect the rent. That is the only time that Bat ever see him.

Bat feel if he keep quiet Charlie might think he not there, or he still sleeping, and go away.

'Open up Battersby,' Charlie say, 'I see you peep by the window.' Bat open the door angrily. 'A man just get up,' he say, 'a man ain't even wash his face yet, nor had breakfast.'

'I can't help for that,' Charlie say. He stand up by the door waiting for an invite to come in. 'You owe two weeks rent. I come round last Sunday but you was out.'

'I am out this Sunday too,' Bat say.

'You know what the rule is,' Charlie say. 'If two weeks go and you don't pay, out. You should praise God that I come, else you don't pay and you get put out.'

'I ain't have no money,' Bat say.

Charlie stop waiting for invitation and come inside, and went and sit down on the bed.

It look like Charlie was up with the larks. The man dress up in a smart suit and a flashy tie, and he have on them new kind of shoes what you can't tell if is boots or shoes. And his hair plaster down with coconut oil and lard, to make it look smooth, though here and there a little kink rebelling.

Just the sight of the man dress up so much so early in the morning put Bat off, not that it needed that. Nobody in Brixton didn't like Charlie. Not only because he was a rent collector, but because he had a way as if butter won't melt in his mouth, and all the time you know the man vicious like a snake and only after your money. Once he collect that rent, Charlie would change as if the pound notes had some sort of chemical what had an effect on him as soon as they touch his hand. If he was serious, his face break out in a grin. If he was standing up, he sit down. As if it had two Charlies, Before-Charlie and After-Charlie.

Right now, it was Before-Charlie who was talking to Battersby.

'I go have to give you notice,' Before say.

'I only have three pounds,' Bat say.

Charlie hesitate between Before and After, but Before win. 'That ain't even one week rent,' he say.

'Look at this bloody place,' Bat say, 'look at this bloody room. It damp, it old, it falling apart. The whole house going to collapse on my head one day.'

'The builders coming in next week,' Charlie say.

'What builders? You been saying that for years now, Charlie. Listen man, you is one of we, you shouldn't be so hard on the boys.'

'I always have to tell all-you that this is my job,' Charlie say. 'I only working for the company, and is my job to go around and collect the rent. But I tell you what I could do. A Jamaican fellar looking for a place, and I could put another bed in here, and bring down your rent to two pounds.'

'I don't want no kiss-me-arse Jamaican living with me,' Bat say.

'When you take this room the first time, we give it to you as a double,' Charlie say. 'It going to make it easier for you.'

'You can't get a Trinidadian instead?'

'Look at you,' Charlie say expansively, 'we have so much of prejudice with the white people and them, and you don't like a fellow-countryman in Brit'n. How we could get on?'

'You know all the answers,' Bat sulk, 'but I know you, Charlie. You would be a missionary to the white races if it pay off.'

'A man got to live,' Charlie say, 'if the world offering that sort of situation, what you want me to do? You want me to change the world?'

'A man got to have things he believe in,' Bat say.

'Well all I believe in, is what bringing me money, because money is the thing that I got to have to live in this world. If you vex with me, what happen? The sun stop shining? Snow stop falling? No. But if I ain't have a job, and if I ain't have money, I might as well be dead, because I can't live without it. What the arse I really care what you think of me? Or anybody else? That don't count at all. If I had a million pounds, you would fall down on your knees and salaam, no matter if you think in your heart that I is a bastard. You think I don't know people?'

'Still, it have a few of we who have principles. Fellars like you, you only out to bleed people, even your own kind.'

'I can't do anything,' Charlie say. 'If you have any complaints, I could tell the company about them, and leave it to the top men to do something.'

'Why you don't look for a decent work,' Bat say, 'instead of robbing poor people.'

Of a sudden Charlie get up, as if he tired talking, and say, 'You agree to another tenant coming or no? Because if you don't, I will write out a notice for you.'

'I mad to get the Rent Tribunal after you-all,' Bat grumble.

'I wouldn't do that if I was you,' Charlie say. 'You remember what happen to Eric Lopley?'

What happen to Eric Lopley was past history, but all the same, nobody ain't ever forget. Eric was a Grenadian who get to share a room in the house. The room had three other fellars in it. Eric wasn't in the country long, and it may be that back in the West Indies he hear about the housing situation for the boys, how landlords like to cram up a room and charge high rent, and how the authorities always complaining. So it may be that he thought all he had to do was go to this Rent Tribunal thing that he hear about, and they would break down the house and build a new one, or something. Anyway, Eric went, and when the Rent Tribunal hear what he had to say, they say they hear of many cases, but this was the worse they ever know. That same night, two Englishers stop Eric in front the house and wash his arse with licks. They beat him until he couldn't move, and left him laying down on the pavement. Eric migrate to Birmingham, saying that London was too evil for him.

The next time Charlie Victor pass around to collect rent, he full of sympathy with the tenants, telling them what a shame it was. 'All the same,' he say, 'let that be a lesson, you see how they against us in this country, so the thing to do is make the best of it. I myself tired talking to the company about getting some repairs done, and thinning out the tenants. You-all mustn't blame me, I only making a living.'

Well Bat remembering all that, and he frighten if the company treat him like Eric Lopley if he go to the Rent Tribunal.

'I was only making a joke,' he say.

'You mustn't make them kind of jokes,' Charlie say. 'Somebody might get to hear.'

Bat don't know what to do. If he give Charlie Victor the three pounds, he would be broken for the rest of the week.

'I tell you what,' he say at last. 'Bring the Jamaican fellar, but don't tell him what the rent is. You just let him come and I will give you six pounds a week, every week, on the dot.'

'That is a bit unusual,' Charlie say.

'Live and let live,' Bat say.

'All right,' Charlie say, 'being as both of we is Trinidadians, I will ease up the situation for you. Shift some of the things you have out of the cupboard, and give him some room.'

* * *

Thus it was that Harry Banjo come to live with Battersby in that basement room in Brixton, and get behind Bat for a set of them to pool together and buy their own house, instead of paying all that wicked rent.

But before we come to that, I best hads tell you some more about Battersby, because he have a sister named Jean, who living in a room upstairs in the same house with another thing from Trinidad name Matilda. To tell you the truth, though Jean was a nice girl, she was a hustler, going up to Hyde Park every evening to look for fares. But Bat don't care what she do. The way he look at it, she have her own life to live, and if she want to hustle fares, that is her own business.

In fact though Bat is the man, was Jean who always taking the upper hand, and after him to go to work, and keep the basement clean, and take his clothes to the laundry, and in general trying to improve Bat as a human being.

Sometimes she come down in the basement and help him to clean up, grumbling all the time, but still doing the work. And the morning after Harry Banjo arrive, she come down. Bat wasn't there, only Harry tuning his banjo.

'What you doing here?' she ask him right away, because she didn't know anything about this new tenant.

'I am living here,' Harry say, strumming the banjo. The way he strumming, as if his fingers reacting to Jean more than his eyes, because Jean was a sharp craft, and though white people feel that the boys only after white things, Harry never see a piece of skin like the one before him now.

'Which part Battersby is?' Jean ask next.

'He gone out,' Harry say. 'Would you like a cup of tea?'

Now all this time Harry Banjo don't know that is Battersby sister he talking to, because Bat didn't tell him anything.

And as for Jean, she so surprise that this man offering her a cuppa, because she always have to slave for Bat and do everything.

'I don't mind,' she say, and sit down by the table, watching Harry put the kettle on by the gas ring near the fireplace. 'You from Jamaica, ain't you?'

'You never hear about me?' Harry say, as if he is some famous film star or something. 'You don't know I am the greatest calypsonion in town?'

Jean sniff. 'Since when you living with Bat?'

'Only yesterday.'

Harry want to tell she that he only land up in the country a few weeks, but he don't want to appear like no newcomer who don't know anything at all. Besides, from the moment he see Jean as if he feel a kind of electric current pass. Right there and then if Jean did tell him to go and jump off of Nelson Column in Trafalgar Square, Harry would of gone. Is so it happen to you sometimes.

'You know Battersby long?' he ask.

Was then that Jean realise that he ain't know that she was Battersby sister. She was mad to keep on fooling him, but she tell him who she was and say that she come to clean up the room. She pick up the banjo and look at it.

'You does make money playing this thing and saying calypso?'

'Not saying, singing,' Harry say.

'All-you Jamaicans don't know calypso,' Jean scoffed. 'Trinidad is the place.'

'Hear you!' Harry say, 'I does make up my own tunes and words.'

'In any case,' she go on, 'them English people won't know the difference.'

As Harry was pouring out the tea, Battersby come back and make a formal introduction.

'I can't clean up if the two of you going to be in the room,' Jean say.

'We could go up in your room and wait till you finish,' Bat say. 'Matilda home?'

Bat had his eye on Matilda for weeks, but she was playing hard-to-get. Bat didn't want to rush the position: he figure if he give she enough rope she might trip up of her own accord.

'You leave Matilda alone,' Jean say, knowing what kind of fellar Bat is. Every time she bring a friend home Bat want to make a stroke with them. She even warn Matilda about him, although she regret afterwards because Matilda perk up and ask all kinds of question, how many girls he have, what job he doing, if he on night-shift or day.

'The way you have this place so damn dirty,' she say looking around. 'And now is two of you.'

'I had a upstairs room the last place I live,' Harry Banjo say, 'and the landlady used to clean it every day. But she was a Jamaican.'

'A lot of you Jamaican buy your own house,' Bat say.

'What stopping you from doing the same thing?' Harry say. 'Why about six of we can't pool and do the same thing? You ain't have friends?'

Now, that is exactly how everything happen. If I was writing a story I could make up all sorts of things, that Bat say so-and-so and Jean say this-and-that and Harry say but-what-about.

Because how you know the idea catch on? Just like that? Is so things happen in life. Some words here, a little meeting there, and next thing you know, War Declare, or a Man Gone to the Moon.

And being as I want to tell the truth, I have to say that that is how it happen.

Bat say, 'I was thinking of that, you know.' (Funny how he never ask the geni on the wallpaper for a house to live in!)

'You ain't the only one thinking,' Jean say, 'but what you going to do? Look at this place! If you add up all the rent we been paying, we could of put down a deposit on a house long time!'

'You give me an idea there, Harry,' Bat say.

'If you really serious, we could do it,' Harry say. 'I for one expect some big money one of these days. My agent tell me to make some recordings on a tape and he would try and sell me. You don't know anybody what have a tape recorder you could borrow?'

'I know somebody,' Jean say.

'Take it easy, now,' Bat say. 'First thing we have to get the boys together and discuss the idea, and see how they react. Is no sense planning anything until we get together.'

* * *

The get together happen a few nights later, right there in the basement room: It had Alfonso, Fitzwilliams, de Nobriga, Sylvester, Gallows, and Poor-me-One.

To introduce you to all these characters would take you into different worlds, don't mind all of them is the same colour! But if you want to start with Poor, he does traffic in dope cigarettes. Nobody don't know which part he does get them from. He have a way of disappearing from the scene for days and weeks, then he reappear as if he was there all the time. And always, the same impression on his face, as if he is a walking statue or painting. Always cool, on top of the world, as if he have a Secret. To go into more detail—tell you where he come from originally, whether he six foot tall or five foot six, whether he have big eyes and a small nose—what difference it make to you? All you interested in is that he black—to English people, every black man look the same. And to tell you he come from Trinidad and not Jamaica—them two places a thousand miles

apart—won't matter to you, because to Englishers the
West Indies is the West Indies, and if a man say he come
from Tobago or St. Lucia or Grenada, you none the wiser.

Next, take Gallows. As he come into the room, you
know what he doing? His head bent down, and Gallows
searching all over the room for a five-pound note that he
lost one day.

Many years ago in Trinidad a calypso make up about
Gallows. What happen was a feller name Johnny thief
Gallows girl, and the calypso quote Gallows as saying,
when he catch up with Johnny, 'The grave for Johnny and
the gallows for me.'

And the five-pound note? Well, one day Gallows lost
this five pound. He went back down the road looking for
it. He search his room. He stop people on the road asking
them if they see his fiver anywhere? To lost a fiver like that
was no joke. It hurtful enough when you have to pay
income tax, or a landlord bleeding you for the rent, or the
boss deducting money for club fund and pension and
insurance and that sort of thing. But to have a fiver disappear just like that, as if it never exist, I mean, that really
hurt Gallows. In his mind he already spend that five
pounds—three for rent, two for rations. Imagine facing a
whole week and not having to worry. And when he discover the fiver missing, he only laugh. The possibility of
that fiver getting lost casually, like falling from his pocket,
was so remote that Gallows was sure he had it in another
pocket, or in a drawer in his room, or—as the search
went on and desperation begin—maybe he lend it to somebody and forget?

Search high, search low, Gallows ain't find that fiver.
And it come like an obsession with him. The more he look
and he ain't find it, the more he come sure that one day he

bound to find it. So all over Londontown Gallows walking as if his head have no support and falling forward, and his eyes scouring the streets. He make some interesting discoveries, like wristwatch and french letters, and once he find a tanner. Gallows so bloody vex when he find the tanner that he fling it away. Tanner! Who want any blasted tanner when a man lose a whole five pound?

And he roam in strange places that he never went before, because with these breezes that does blow over the city, you never know, one might lift up the fiver from one district and blow it into another, in somebody yard, or through an open window or something.

So as Gallows come in Battersby room he ain't even say a word to anybody, he just begin to bend, looking under the bed, under the table, shifting the girls' legs (because Poor and Alfonso bring their girls with them) and then looking around the room, as if the fiver might be stuck up on the wall or the ceiling.

Meantime mine host gone out with Harry Banjo to buy some soda water and lime juice, because they already had a bottle of rum what remain from what Harry bring from Jamaica, and naturally they have to warm the boys up with a few drinks before making the preposition about the house.

Listen to Harry Banjo, as he and Bat going to the off-licence: 'How them fellars have white girls, boy?' Is the sort of question you get regularly from the islanders who fresh in Londontown, like 'How you get to Piccadilly,' or 'Which part I could get a room to rent.'

'Is the attraction of opposites,' Bat say. 'You want one? Just let me know and I will put you on to a nice thing living by Clapham Junction.'

'I like Jean,' Harry say.

'Jean is fire,' Bat say.

Meanwhile back at the basement, the boys getting restless. Poor light up a weed and start to smoke.

Alfy say, 'You better stop smoking that cigarette here. You know Bat don't like it.'

'You want a quick drag?' Poor ask him, and pass the weed. Everybody in the room had a drag before it get back to Poor.

Jean and Matilda come down from upstairs. Jean had a tape recorder under she arm. As soon as Poor see Jean he nip the cigarette and push the butt in his pocket.

Jean sniff. 'Who smoking weed?'

Everybody keep quiet.

'Which one of you it is?' she say, looking at Poor. 'I tired warning you all this thing is serious trouble.'

Poor say, maliciously, 'some people get kicks one way, and others another way.'

'Is nobody else but you, Poor.' Jean put the tape recorder on the table and face him arms akimbo. 'You better don't smoke any more in this room.'

'Just because you know the difference between "long time" and "short time" you don't have to get on so,' Poor say.

'What I do is my business,' Jean say.

'And what I do is mine,' Poor say.

It looks like the two of them was going to start a big quarrel but lucky thing same time Bat and Harry come back. Bat open up Harry bottle of rum and pass around some drinks. Harry play generous with one of the last packs of cigarettes he had remaining from what he bring off the ship, and pass it around. By the time it reach back it almost empty.

Jean say, 'It have ash trays all about, don't flick no ashes on the ground, eh, is I who have to clean this room out.'

Well everybody find a place to sit down—some of the girls

on the fellars laps—and they start up on this bottle of rum. It didn't matter to any of them why Battersby call for this meeting as long as the rum was flowing. In fact the bottle get down in short pants before Poor say, 'Let we hear about this plan you have, man, me and Lily want to go to the pictures.'

'Yes yes, is time to get serious,' Bat say. 'Now listen. I ain't want to make no big speeches. Everybody know what hell it is to get a place to live, and the idea is to start saving up some money, and we put it together and buy a house.'

'That is a highly original idea,' Fitz say, 'you think of it all by yourself?'

'I want the basement,' Gallows say, as if the house buy already.

'I want the ground floor,' de Nobriga say, 'I tired climbing stairs.'

'You see the same thing?' Bat raise his hands complaining to everybody. 'Everything is a joke, laugh kiff-kiff. That is why we could never progress.'

'I ain't laughing,' Sylvester say.

* * *

Now, I will have to digress with a ballad about Syl, which will help to explain why Syl ain't laughing. In the first place, you mightn't think that Syl is an Indian, because he ain't have a Indian name, and a lot of people don't know it have true-true Indians living in the West Indies. Not Carib Indians or Red Indians, but Indians from India, wearing sari and thing. But some of them get so westernise that they don't even know where the Ganges is, and they pick up all sort of fancy name instead of the usual Singh or Ram. That's how Syl name Sylvester. He had a habit of knocking wood for luck, and kissing the Cross, but I will tell you more about that later.

One time Syl was catching real hell to get a room. He

walking all over town reading the notice boards in the sweet shops and tobacconists, but all he could see is 'No Kolors' or 'Sorry, Uropean only.' Syl was thinking how is a hell of a thing these people don't want him, when they can't even spell.

Well while he stand up there, the old Bat stroll along.

'What happening?' Bat say.

'I was looking for a place to live, man,' Syl say.

'You won't find nothing on them boards,' Bat say. 'But seeing that both of we is Trinidadians together, I will tell you of a place. Right up there by the next block, it have a house with a English landlord who taking Indians. He don't want any West Indians, mark you, but he taking real Indians. You could go there and try.'

'But I am from the West Indies,' Syl say.

'Nevertheless,' Bat say, 'You are an Indian. Why you don't go and try?'

'I don't too like living with a set of Indian people,' Syl grumble. 'So much of curry and dhal and *kia-san-hai*.'

'Well, is up to you,' Bat say.

In the end, after looking at some more notices, Syl decide to go to this house Bat tell him about. He knock at the door and stand up waiting for the landlord.

The landlord come and look at Syl suspiciously. 'Yes?' he say, as if Syl ask him a question and he answering 'yes.'

'I am straight from the banks of the Ganges,' Syl say. 'I am a student from the Orient seeking a roof over my head.'

'You are not wearing your national garments,' the landlord say.

'When you are in Rome,' Syl shrug.

'What part of India do you come from?'

'West India.'

'What is your name?'

'Ram Singh Ali Mohommed—Esquire,' Syl say.

'I don't know,' the Englisher hedging. 'What are you a student of?'

'I am a student of life,' Syl say stoutly, and add, for good measure, 'Are we not all?'

Same time, as the two of them stand there talking, a Indian tenant come to go inside. This test have a big beard and he wearing turban.

'*Acha, bhai,*' he say gravely to Syl, and at the same time he clasp his hands together across his chest.

'Er—acha, acha,' Syl say, and then remembering some of them Indian dishes he see in a restuarant, 'aloo, vindallo, dansak, and chutney.'

The fellar give Syl a funny look and went inside.

Well this English landlord give Syl a room, but Syl like he living on hot coals, having to hide from this other Indian fellar (who also say his name is Ram) every time he see him, in case he start up with some kia-san-hai talk. In fact, this Ram looking at Syl so supicious that Syl feel he had to do something about it.

One evening Syl went down to the landlord and say, 'This chap Ram, I don't believe he is from Indian at all.'

'What do you mean,' the landlord say. 'He is a good ten-ant, he has been with me some months now.'

'I am from the Orient,' Syl say, 'and I can tell a pretender when I see one. In the first place he does not sleep with his head to the East. And another thing he is always chanting in his room and creating a nuisance to the other tenants.'

'I will have to do something then,' the Englisher say.

'You don't want to cause discomfort to all the others because of one man,' Syl say.

'Quite so,' the landlord say, 'thank you for telling me.'

'Not at all,' Syl say, 'I like it here.'

And with that Syl relax, because he had no doubt the landlord would cant this Ram out of the house, and he would be able to settle down in peace.

But bam! a few evenings later, as Syl sitting down on the bed, he hear a knocking at the door.

'Just a minute,' Syl say, and he run in the corner and stand up on his head. 'You can come in now,' he say.

The landlord come in. 'What are you doing?' he ask.

'I am practising my yoghourt,' Syl say.

'I have had a word with Mr Ram,' the Englisher say, 'and it is now obvious that you are the one who is not from India.'

Syl come off his head and stand on his feet. 'Are you talking about Mother India?' he say.

'No,' the landlord say, 'I am talking about you having a week's notice. You are flying under false colours, you are from the West Indies. I cannot stand those immigrants, I am sorry to say.'

'You are looking at me,' Syl say, 'a born Indian who grew up on the banks of the Ganges and worked on the rice and tea plantations, and calling me a West Indian?'

'Yes,' the landlord say. 'You look like an Indian, but you are from the same islands as those immigrants. You will have to go.'

'Oh God, places so hard to get.' Syl revert back to West Indian talk. 'You can't give me a chance?'

'I am sorry,' the landlord say. 'Mr Ram has confirmed that you are not from the East.'

'I used to live in the East End,' Syl say hopefully.

'That is not far enough East,' the Englisher say. 'Take a week's notice as from today.'

Well a week later Syl chance to meet Battersby and give him the story. 'If it wasn't for that damn Ram,' he say, 'a man would of still had a place to live.'

'Wait a minute,' Bat say, 'is a fellar with a big beard, and he always wearing a turban?'

'That is the scamp,' Syl say.

'Man,' Bat say, 'that is a fellar from Jamaica what I send to the same house for a room!'

*   *   *

So to come back to the basement in Brix, that is one of the reasons why Syl wasn't laughing when Bat talk about buying this house.

And although it look like the boys making joke, in fact all of them thinking serious about the idea.

'We have to give up a lot of things,' Bat say, 'because I know it ain't easy to save. For one thing, I feel everybody should give up smoking. Another, no drinking. Another, no spending money on women.'

The fellars silent as they contemplate this lark.

'Them is some big request,' Nobby say. 'Who going to know if somebody smoke and drink?'

'I go watch out for them!' Gallows say. 'And if I catch anybody smoking or drinking or going theatre I report to you, Battersby!'

Old Gallows feel he had to say something, because he ain't have no work and he living catch-as-catch-can. Otherwise they might leave him out.

'You could always trust old Gallows,' Fitz say sarcastic.

'Anybody you catch, charge them two and six!' Gallows went on, as if the idea have him excited.

'We have to trust one another,' Bat say. 'We have to treat this thing serious, else it won't work at all, and if anybody feel they can't manage they best hads drop out now.'

Bat look around. Poor raise his hand and say, 'You always up to some scheme, Bat. Tell me, who going to hold the money?'

'Well is I who organising everything,' Bat say. 'Who you expect?'

'I don't like this idea,' Poor say, 'you better count me out.'

'I will be the treasurer,' Jean cut in, 'if you all don't trust Battersby with the money.'

'Anybody else want to drop out?' Bat ask.

Alfy, Nobby, Fitz and Sylvester look at one another.

'Harry Banjo in this thing too?' Nobby ask.

'Is I who bring up the idea,' Harry say. 'All you Trinidadians can't think for yourself.'

'Trust these Jamaicans,' Fitz mutter.

'Well I for one agree with the idea, if you all serious,' Syl say.

'You Alfy?' Bat ask.

'Yes.'

'You Nobby?'

'Yes.'

'Fitz?'

'All right, we give it a try. But if everything turn old mask I want my money back right away.'

'That make six of we,' Bat say. 'Should be enough.'

'Aye man, what about me?' Gallows ask anxiously, 'ain't you counting me in? Seven is a lucky number.'

'All right,' Bat say, more to avoid argument than anything else, because he sure Gallows won't be able to contribute anything.

Poor get up and turn to Lily. 'Come girl, let we go, I not interested in this deal at all. And if I was all you fellars,' he say to the boys, 'I think twice before parting with any money. Them people who have house to sell don't want to sell to black man.'

'A lot of fellars have houses,' Harry say.

'Yes, but which part?' Poor say. 'In all them back streets

where the sun don't shine, in some tumbledown old house what only have a year to stand again.'

'Don't bother with Poor,' Bat say, 'he only beginning to feel jealous how he drop out. Just wait until we get a mansion and he would wish he was in it.'

When Poor and Lily left, Harry go to the tape recorder and open it.

'Take care with that,' Jean say, 'it ain't mine.'

'You going to record something?' Nobby ask.

'Yes,' Harry say. 'I going to do some calypsoes and sell. I bet in the end I put more money than any of you in that house!'

By this time, with the rum and the talking, all of them feeling good, and imagining some big house that they could have a flat in, and ain't have no landlord or landlady ready to throw you out. Gallows come and start to fiddle around the tape recorder, but Jean give his hand ONE slap.

Alfy and Syl finish off the bottle of rum, putting a little bit in each of the glasses.

'This is the last drink you fellars having,' Gallows warn them. 'After tonight, any man I catch smoking or drinking will have to pay two and six. Not so Bat?'

'If you catch them,' Bat say.

Fitz blow smoke in Gallows face and say, 'As for you, you will be so busy looking for your lost fiver, you won't have time to notice anything else.'

And hear old Bat with Matilda, 'You know you could always come and live with me—and Jean—when we get the new house.'

'The day I live with you is when we get married—if we get married,' Matilda tell him.

'That could happen too,' Bat say, his brain sweeten up with the rum.

Fitz happen to hear Bat say that, and he say, 'Boy, don't get in no married business you hear!'

Bat laugh at Fitz. 'I will take your advice, Fitz,' he say, 'because if it ever have a man who should know, is you.'

In a little while I will give the ballad about Fitz, what make Bat tell him that, because right now Harry Banjo shaping up with his instrument to sing calypso, as Jean have the tape ready, and Nobby push the plug in a socket by the wall. As soon as Jean switch on bam! the fuse blow and the lights went out.

'Jesus Christ,' Bat say, 'fix the fuse quick Harry before somebody start to make noise.'

No sooner said than a shrill voice come pelting down from upstairs: 'Mr. Battersby! Are you tampering with the electricity again?'

Battersby start to swear. 'Go on Harry, the fuse box in the passageway. Jean, go with him and show him.'

A lot of tittering and giggling going on in the dark, nobody thinking of striking a match, least of all Bat, who make a wild grab for Matilda in the dark and had she on his lap.

Outside Jean strike a match and Harry follow she out in the passageway. Deciding to make hay while the match was shining, Harry say: 'I can't get a chance with you alone at all, Jean. It look like you avoiding me.'

'I ain't have no time with you, man,' Jean say. 'Make haste and fix the fuse.'

She pick up a piece of newspaper and light it to save matches as Harry open the fusebox.

'Come and go for a walk afterwards,' Harry urge.

'I have my work to do.'

'I don't understand this night work that you have,' Harry say, as he change the fuse wire. 'Which part it is? Where you working, in a factory.'

Jean laugh. 'You could call it a kind of open-air factory.'

'And what you have to do?'

Jean laugh again. 'You could say I is a kind of receptionist. I have to entertain the customers, and make sure they satisfy.'

Harry frown. 'I don't know why you getting on so cagey with me,' he grumble. 'You know I like you, from that first morning when you come in the basement. You know my uncle wanted me to married a girl in Kingston before I come?'

'In truth?'

'Yes.'

'And why you didn't?'

'Maybe because I was waiting for somebody like you.'

'Do tell. Go on, you will soon meet white girls.'

'I won't marry none of them, though.'

All this talk sweetening up Jean, because it was a lonely life in London, and many times she feel to go back home and get some man who would married she. Now she was thinking, why not Harry? But she didn't want to sound encouraging.

'Come and go back,' she say, as Harry finish the fuse.

'One of these days you will come out with me, eh Jean?' he ask.

'Yes, when cock have teeth.'

But she allow Harry to put his hand on her shoulder as they going back in: after all, she shouldn't play too hard to get, it might put him off completely.

Back in the room, a big contention going on, because when the lights come back on suddenly Bat find Gallows on the other side of Matilda, and he want to know what the arse he doing there, if he expect to find the lost fiver stick up underneath Matilda arm?

Anyway, order get restored, and everybody waiting to hear Harry Banjo who tuning and tuning as if he looking for the lost chord to make a start.

Hear Nobby: 'That guitar had its days.'

And Syl: 'Is not a guitar, stupid, is a mandolin.'

And Alfy: 'Don't express your ignorances, it is a ukulele.'

But Fitz say, 'What I want to know is if Harry Banjo could sing calypso.'

Harry settle that point by beginning to sing, after Bat call for silence from everybody. To tell the truth, Harry wasn't so bad. I mean, them kind of singing that you hear these days, you could rate Harry. He sing four songs. He sing Old Lady You Mashing My Toe, Stone-cold Dead in the Market, The Weatherman Lying, and he sing one that he make up himself, call Brit'n, Lovely Brit'n.

But when they do the playback, Gallows and Nobby was whispering in the background for one of the numbers, and they had was to record that one again.

'All you like children,' Bat say. 'You know the man doing a recording. Well all right, you can't keep quiet until he finish?'

'It wasn't me,' Gallows say, 'it was Nobby who saying he could sing better than Harry.'

On that Harry push the mike close to Nobby and hand him the banjo. 'Here, sing,' he say, but Nobby back down, saying that wasn't what he was saying at all, that what he was saying was Harry should of electrify the banjo.

'And further more,' Nobby went on, 'these days all kinds of fellars singing shit and playing guitar, you think a black man would stand a chance?'

'That's the reason none of you getting any place,' Harry say. 'You all just sit down on your arse and moan and wonder. You just wait till I sign up a contract, you will have to call me Mister then.'

'You right boy Harry,' Jean side with him. 'These fellars is a set of scallywags, all they could do is waste time, gamble, and chase women. They ain't have no ambition.'

Well seeing the bottle of rum was finish, and the discussion, everybody get up to go. Jean and Matilda went back upstairs.

Hear Bat at the door, to the boys, 'Keep thinking about the house. No more living in cramp-up room paying exorbited rent. That will help to keep you out of temptation.'

'Don't worry Bat,' Gallows say, 'I will watch out for who squandering money and report them. Drop them out of the scheme if they can't give up some vices for a house to live in! And don't forget I bags the basement, eh?'

When only Bat and Harry was left, Bat say, 'I don't know, these fellars as if they not so serious about this thing at all.'

Harry say, 'We will wait and see. Give it a chance. How much so you think we going to need for a deposit?'

'About two-three hundred.'

Harry whistle. 'That is a lot of money.'

'I was surprised to see Fitz,' Bat say.

'Why?'

'He have a wife there who don't let him go out at all.'

'I didn't know he was married.'

Bat chuckle. 'Was a big thing. Let me give you the ballad . . .'

*　*　*

Boy, (Bat telling Harry) is a true saying that if your mouth big, your head small. Because the way Fitz used to get on about women, you feel that he would be the last man in the world to get married. We used to go round by Nobby to play a little rummy, you see, and coast a few beers and old-talk and thing. And you should hear Fitz when we talking about birds.

'Boy, woman! Not me! They too malicious!'

'How you mean they malicious?' Nobby say, because

although everybody accustom to hearing this same tune from Fitz, Nobby like to crank him up.

'Well you know what I mean. The thing is, you have to know how to treat them. I am a professor of womanology, boy. If I had five little fingers, I could wrap them around all of them.'

'Well look how Alfy girl going around with another fellar,' Nobby say, giving him a little push after the crank. 'What you would do, if you was in his place?'

'Do?' Fitz shake the cards in his hand like a caveman shaking a club. 'I beat she like a snake. All woman want is blows to keep them quiet. One time I was going around with a thing from Croydon, and she wanted to married me. I say, "Look here, girl, don't mention that word again, don't even think it in your head, where I can't see or hear!" She say, "You can't stop me from thinking." I say, "No, but I could damage your thinking-box!" And with that I ups and give she ONE clout behind she head, and I must have knock the word clean out, because she never mention married again.'

'Is all right with the girls back home,' Alfy say, 'but this bird is English.'

'So what?' Fitz say, 'all of them the same.'

'Woman does always cause trouble,' Nobby say, stoking fire to keep Fitz going. 'I mean, look how we easy, not a worry in the world. We playing a little rummy, we have some bitter to drink, and it have some peas and rice in the pot if anybody want.'

'That is life,' Fitz say. 'But even if it had woman here, so what? Who is them? Take me. If I had a wife here, now, and she nudging me and saying, "Time to go home, Fitz," or "Don't drink so much beer, Fitz," you know what I do? I only look at her, that's all. Just look.'

And Fitz put down his cards and look at Nobby as how

he would of look at his wife if he had one. 'I wouldn't have to say a word, I wouldn't have to make a move. In fact,' and here he pick up his cards again, 'the situation would never arise!'

And that was the way the talk used to go whenever woman was the topic, and all of we used to think that Fitz would rather dead than get married.

Well papa, things was going along like that until bam! Nobby cousin Teena, who was living in Willesden, get put out and had to come and stay by him.

'Look at my crosses,' Nobby moaning to the boys.

And hear Fitz: 'Throw she out! Why she had to come by you? She couldn't get a room somewhere else?'

'All good things come to an end,' Alfy say.

'I know she going and make misery,' Nobby say 'she always getting on like a boss and want me to do this and do that.'

'Look at him!' Fitz say. 'You must be like me. Treat them like the old Bogart, rough and tough.'

Well in truth and in fact, Teena really begin to stick like a leech behind poor Nobby from the time she come. Everytime we having a session of cards she want to break the party up.

This time so, hear Fitz: 'Woman, you could tell Nobby what you want, but don't interfere with me at all at all, else is big trouble in this room.'

And listen to Teena: 'I don't like the company you keeping, Nobby, these fellars only encouraging you to idle.'

And poor Nobby: 'Yes Teena, no Teena, all right Teena.'

One evening we just settling down to a nice little session when she come in.

'Nobby!' she say, 'you gambling? That is all you have to do in your spare time?'

'We just having a little rummy, Teen,' Nobby say.

'This kind of thing got to stop!' she say. 'I tell you gambling is a vice. And who buy all that beer?'

But hear Fitz! 'Woman, why the hell you don't leave we men alone and go and take a bath or something?'

'You better stop encouraging my cousin in evil ways,' Teena tell him. 'You look like the worse of the lot.'

Well you should know that we had to change the venue for the rummy, and we begin to go round by Alfy room to play. You could imagine how Fitz getting on now. He only holding forth on the evils of woman, and saying that none of them in this world could ever treat him like how Teena treating Nobby, and if he was Nobby he would ups one day and give she two-three cuff between she eyes, or a high fall.

A-a! Gradually my boy begin to simmer down, until a time come when he change key.

One day he say, 'This Teena is a big joker, *oui.*'

Another day he say, 'I notice Teena have a nice figure you know, she does walk like a wave moving in deep water.'

And the next thing you know, one evening we spot him and Teena coasting around Piccadilly Circus, holding hands! You know the excuse he give? He say that Teena don't know Londontown at all, and he showing her the high spots!

Well about two weeks after that bam! Fitz went and get married to Teena! Wonders will never cease, I tell you, I for one would have bet a hundred pounds Fitz would never get stick.

Anyway, a few evenings after we went round by Fitz carrying some beer and two new packs of cards for a session. When we get there, we find Teena sewing and Fitz washing pot and pan in the sink.

'I ain't feeling too good tonight, boys,' he say, 'I have a bad headache, I can't play.'

A few nights later we went back again. This time Fitz scrubbing the floor. And hear him as he give us a worm's eye look: 'I really busy tonight, boys. It look as if you all always choosing the wrong time.'

It look so in truth! Because every time we go by Fitz for a game, he either scrubbing or washing or sweeping. And all this time, Teena only looking at we, ain't saying a word, just rocking in a rocking chair and keeping an eye on Fitz to make sure he don't sweep no dust under the carpet.

He even stop going out: we can't see him anywhere at all. Next thing you know, somebody spot Fitz in the park pushing pram!

And today he have three picc'ns, and is a wonder we see him here tonight, Teena must of heard we planning to buy a house and send him to find out what happening.

* * *

That was the ballad that Bat give Harry about Fitz, killing himself with laugh as he say it. After that Harry went out somewhere—the few drinks sweeten him up and he thought he might go round by a friend he had in Somerleyton Road.

Bat sit down alone by the table thinking. When you get accustom to living by yourself, it hard to have somebody with you. True Harry was paying more rent than he should without knowing anything. But many times Bat wish he was still alone. In one dream period he even wonder what would happen if Harry find out about the Aladdin lamps on the wallpaper, and want to rub them and try out his luck. It even reach a stage where he looking on the basement room with affection. Now that he was sharing it, it didn't look so bad, a dash of paint here, a few nails there, some plaster on the ceiling, and it might look as good as any room that the boys living in. After all, he have his own entrance, don't mind them stinking dustbin in the way. To have your own entrance was a great thing, you could bring any amount of birds in without anybody else in the house knowing your business. He might even number it 13A, as he see some houses do, and then the postman would bring letters direct to him.

But with the plan to buy a house, at last it look as if he had something constructive in mind. He didn't know how things would work out, but if the boys get serious, you never can tell, maybe they really get a mansion to live in. And also with all the joking, if Harry lucky and some of them show business people like his voice, who could tell what and what mightn't happen?

Is so life was, you had to take chances, and one day your luck might turn. And if you yourself ain't have anything to offer, it good to stick with fellars like Harry, and Alfy and Syl and the rest of the boys. All of we can't be blight, Bat think, out of six seven fellars, one bound to be lucky, something good bound to happen to one of we. Bat ain't care who it happen to, as long as he around to share in the good fortune.

*   *   *

Is a funny thing, but men have a lot of thoughts and ideas what sleeping inside and never get a chance to come out. If for instance you notice a fellar who quiet and easy with a job that bringing him in about ten quid a week, you put a hundred pounds in his hand and you will see a different man. You might look at this fellar and say he ain't have no ambition, he look so satisfy with this ten quid a week. And bam! you put this hundred quid in his hand, and all them thoughts and ideas what was sleeping yawn and come wide awake. Suddenly this same fellar realise he want a car, or a yacht, or a platinum blonde. Mark you, is not the money what create these ideas: he had them all the time, but only now they getting a chance to breathe. Things will always change for a man if he get a break. It ain't in reality have anything like a rut: if a fellar in a rut break his hand, suddenly he thinking new thoughts, he wondering what he would do if he have to go hospital and they cut off his hand: he imagining himself doing everything with one hand: is as if he facing life for the first time.

When Gallows left number 13A (let we number Battersby basement for him, he will feel good) he walk away as if he drifting on a cloud. As if the plan to buy a house make a new man of him. In all his life, Gallows never had a plan, never had ideas about the future.

Gallows reach England by accident. In Port of Spain harbour one night, where he was a stevedore, he was down in the bottom of a ship which was loading up. One of the crates what had rum in it fall down and break open and rum start flowing all about. Fellars gone mad looking for old tins and cups or anything that wouldn't leak: Gallows find a bucket and full it up with rum.

That is all Gallows remember until he wake up about a day after. He hearing a noise thum, thum, thum and he thought he had a heavy headache until he realise it was a engine. What engine? Suddenly Gallows jump up from where he was laying down between two crates, wondering where he was and what the arse happening? They charge him for stowing away when the ship reach Plymouth, and he serve a month and afterwards drift up to Londontown, hungry and destitute. He get in with a big, blowsy thing from Scandinavia who had all she front teeth missing. Every time she talk, she putting she hand up to her mouth to hide the space, as if fingers could substitute for teeth. And she was always surprise at how many coloured people in London.

You could imagine this big, blowsy thing, putting she hand up to her mouth, and saying with a lisp, 'So many black ones!' as she walking in Oxford Street.

Nevertheless, if it wasn't for this dilapidated sleeper, Gallows would of catch his royal arse, because he didn't have no work, (a), and he didn't have no place to live, (b), and he didn't know nobody in the city, (c).

The sleeper had a room in one of them big, posh houses in Hampstead where she was working as a maid. Gallows used to hide in this room, and she used to bring food for him. As long as Gallows belly full and he had a place to sleep, he didn't think about tomorrow. Then the lady of the house catch them one day, and out! Gallows find himself adrift in Londontown. He make his way down to Brixton with the last two and six he had. Somehow he figure out that that was the safest district to go to, that he bound to meet some fellow countryman who would ease up the situation, give him some shelter and a meal.

And as luck would have it, a Jamaican fellar what had a club give him work to clean it out, and say he could sleep in the club for a couple of nights until he get a place. It was in this same club that he get to meet the other boys, because he was always hanging around. Gallows was the sort of fellar who had to attach himself to other men. Left on his own, he didn't know what to do. If a fellar tell Gallows come and go up the road for a walk, he going. If a fellar say come and go and look for woman, Gallows going. As if, by himself, he can't exist, life too big for him to tackle, he can't get any ideas, he can't do anything, he can't plan what he going to do tomorrow.

All day long he liming around the Brixton market looking for somebody he know, somebody who might have an idea of what to do with so much of time, how to occupy one day until a next day come.

The loss of the fiver was a good thing in a way, as he had something to do looking for it. But the biggest thing that ever happen to Gallows, bigger even than God, was this idea that the boys come up with to buy a house. To Gallows, if a man have a house he establish his right to live, and he didn't mind even if he had a tenth of a share, or a twentieth for that matter, he would still feel he is the sole owner.

As the days go by and the idea take possession of him, he get to believe that the whole thing was his idea, and that if he don't supervise the show, nothing would happen. Between looking for the fiver and thinking about the house Gallows time was fully occupied. If it wasn't one it was the other. In fact, scouring the streets in the everlasting quest, sometimes his mind drift to mansions and bungalows and cottages, and he had to go back and start to search again.

The biggest kicks was when he passing some of them estate agents office, and it have photos of houses for sale in the window, and some heavy prices like twenty and thirty thousand pounds. Gallows stand up there jingling a few coppers in his pocket as if he had a million or so to spare, and wondering what to do with it.

The first day he go into a office, the agent tell him, 'Frankly, none of my clients desire to sell their property to coloured people. I'm sorry.'

But that was no hurdle for Gallows. He went to another one, and hear him this time: 'H'mm. Not so bad. How much you say? Five thousand? I was really looking for a place for about twenty or so. What about up in Hampstead? Or a Mayfair property?'

And so the dream went on. Standing on the pavement, chuckling to himself, he talk to the notices in the window.

And hear him talking to his friends: 'I going to buy a house, you know.'

'In truth boy?'

'Yes man.'

'When?'

'Well I not in any great hurry. I want to get one in a good locality, where it ain't have so many spades.'

'I never thought you had money, Gallows.'

'Well, I might bring in one or two fellars to share with me, if I can't raise enough.'

Meantime he ain't doing one bloody thing about saving, or anything concrete to make the dream come true. One Saturday afternoon, as he think about it, he decide he better do something else Battersby might drop him out of the scheme. He know the boys does be liming regularly every Saturday around the market, so he went out to spy. First fellar he spot is Alfy. Alfy leaning on a wall, with a camera strap on his shoulder. One time a Englisher tell Alfy how he was walking down the road and a accident happen with two bus and lucky thing he had a camera and he take a snap of it, and sell it for plenty money to the newspapers.

'In truth?' Alfy ask.

'I don't tell lies like you people,' the Englisher say.

Right away Alfy went and buy a camera and begin to take photo left right and centre. And no kind of amateur work, either. When Alfy taking photo, is a big thing. You have to pose in such and such a position, you have to bend and twist and look up and down and sideways until Alfy satisfy that he have the proper angle. This time so, Alfy himself doing all sorts of contortions, he holding the camera sideways, upways, downways, and he squinting one eye and then the other, and he kneeling down and bending over and twisting and turning as if he in agony. And the adjustments! He clicking this button and that on the camera, as if he preparing to let off a atom bomb. Then after all the paraffle he suddenly say 'HOLD IT!' and he catch you with your mouth wide open or scratching your arse or something.

Gallows do as if he ain't see Alfy, and went in the market, certain that by and by he would see all the others he was after.

Sure enough, Sylvester join Alfy, and Poor walk across from the market crowds to join them. Poor moving furtively, as if the police after him or something, his hands in his pocket. Poor always have his hands in his pocket, as if inside them he holding on to something what give him inspiration to continue living.

Alfy call to him: 'What happening, Poor? I am dying for a cigarette, but the old Gallows dodging in and out only waiting for somebody to smoke so he could report to Battersby.'

Now, I want to make it clear that when the boys leave the conference at number 13A, all of them (except Gallows) was looking on the whole scheme as a lark, and had no intention of stopping smoking or drinking to save money for no house. You could imagine how they was thinking when Battersby come up with the idea. This is Nobby: 'H'mm, what shit is this? But let me see what the others will say.' And Syl: 'Ha-ha, these fellars will never get together, but still, let me see who and who will agree.' And Fitz: 'This is my chance if the boys serious.' As for Alfy: 'I will go along and see how things go.'

The point is, that all of them cagey. When they alone they conducting their lives as per usual, but when they get together, they don't know how to behave. No one want to say outright, 'To arse with that idea,' and carry on.

Was only Poor who say flat that he ain't in all that. So now, he say to Alfy: 'Fug Gallows man, look I have some chargers here. You want one? They going cheap, only two and six. As if you all fraid to smoke? As is you I make it two shillings.'

But Alfy was looking at Syl, because after all it didn't matter what Poor want to do, Syl was in the house-buying lark.

Syl say to Poor, 'Boy, you brave, *oui*. You ain't fraid to sell them thing around here? I bet the law catch up with you.'

'They been trying to for a long time,' Poor brag, and he light up a weed and blow the smoke in Syl face.

'You give up smoking Alfy?' Syl ask, hopeful that Alfy would say no. But at the same time Alfy feel that if he say no, Syl might feel he ain't have no guts to save for the house.

So hear Alfy: 'Yes man, and I was able to save more than a pound. You?'

Syl ain't do one arse about saving, but hear him: 'It ain't have nothing in giving up smoking. I ain't touch a fag for weeks.'

Nobby appear on the scene, and though he too dying for a smoke, he don't know how to broach the subject. He tackle it this way: 'You have any cigarettes on you Syl?'

'I give up smoking,' Syl say, as if he offended.

'The whole set of you lying as if you fraid one another,' Poor say. 'I see everyone of you smoking already.'

'Well anyway,' Alfy say, 'I change my brand. I only carrying Woods now—and filter tip, too besides!'

That encourage Syl to say: 'I give up, but I does smoke one now and then.'

And that encouraged Nobby to haul out a pack and pass it around. All the same, he say: 'I putting in some heavy overtime these days. I manage to save three pounds,' as if that entitled him to smoke.

Hear Alfy as he take one: 'I don't know if I should, you know.'

And Syl: 'Well, this is my first for the week.'

As soon as all of them was lighted and taking some big drag right down to the bottom of their lungs, Gallows dart out the crowd in the market. To tell truth, the boys was feeling a little guilty and from the time they spot Gallows everybody nip their cigarette and put their hands behind their backs.

'I seen a lot of smoke over here,' Gallows say as he come up. 'In fact, from the time I see all of you, I feel you was congregating for something evil. Is always suspicious when you together.'

'This is a free country,' Nobby say. 'It so free that even a character like you could move around in peace. Why you don't go and look for your fiver, Gallows?'

'I see smoke!' Gallows repeat, as if he playing landan-tweet-tweet-tweet, a game children does play in the West Indies where they have to find something that hide. 'Which one of you it was?' He ignoring Poor. 'That is why we could never get on in this world. A little thing like smoking you all can't give up to get a decent house to live in.'

'Why you don't go and fug a keyhole?' Poor say.

'I can't trust any of you,' Gallows mutter. He know that if he report them to Battersby they would deny that they was smoking, so what was the use? If Alfy was honest he could of ask him to take a snap whenever anybody smoking. Still, it was a good thing he was around to keep an eye on them, otherwise they spend all their money on fags and drinks. 'You know,' he change the topic, 'ever since that day when I lost my fiver I have a feeling that is one of you who have it. I look all over London and I can't find it.'

'Never mind,' Nobby say, 'one of these days you bound to find it.'

'You really think so Nobby?' Gallows was anxious for some consolation.

'Sure,' Nobby say. 'London is a big place. You only searching in the West End every night, but what about the East End, what about all up by Palmers Green and round by Willesden and Cricklewood and all of them places? You never notice the wind blowing in that direction?'

'You know what I think?' Alfy say. 'I think that fiver fall in the river Thames and get drown.'

'No man,' Nobby say, 'it must be in some drain or other, and he will find it.'

'Is all well and good for you fellars to laugh,' Syl say, 'but is poor Gallows fiver what get lost.'

'Tell them Syl, tell them,' Gallows say.

'Don't mind them, boy Gallows,' Syl say. 'What you doing about the house? You save anything?'

'I am a hard worker, I have money save,' Gallows say. 'I bet in the end I have more than all of you put together!'

'How much you save?' Alfy ask.

'You don't mind. When the time come, I will have my share. Besides, my grandmother ailing in Tobago, she might kick off any day now and leave some money for me.'

'You better pray she dead in time,' Poor say.

'In any case Bat promise me a room,' Gallows say. 'He tell me to keep an eye on you all: I like a hawk these days. You all should be thankful I come just in time to stop you from smoking. You think I fall off a tree? You think I didn't see when Nobby pass the pack around? Imagine if all of you had to pay two and six for breaking the regulations. We could buy a few bricks for the house.'

'You too malicious,' Nobby say. 'One day somebody will chook out your eyes and stuff up your ears.'

'Anyway,' Gallows say, 'I give everybody warning. I

done see Harry Banjo in the market and he was smoking, and I warn him let that be the last time. I feel sorry for him.'

'Why?' Poor demand. 'Ain't all of we is sufferers?'

'Yes, but Harry in love. In love bad with Jean. I don't think he know she is a hustler.'

'You is the best man to tell him,' Alfy suggest.

But Nobby say, 'No, leave the man alone and let him find out for himself. Don't interfere in any man business is my motto.'

Gallows was just about to leave them when he glance down the road and spot Harry coming.

Hear Gallows: 'Hold everything! Look for yourself! Witness Harry smoking. Watch him over there, coming this way. You can't say you didn't see. ALL RIGHT HARRY! I GOT YOU THIS TIME!'

Harry come up and say, 'This was the last cigarette I had from Jamaica, I was just taking a quick draw.'

'Don't bother with Gallows man,' Syl say. 'You have any more? Make a good search. You never know, perhaps one or two fall out the pack and inside loose in your pocket . . . ah, you see!'

'You ain't even finish smoking the one I give you and you sponging on the man,' Nobby say.

By this time everybody light up and smoking, blowing smoke in Gallows face.

Gallows wouldn't give up. 'That is why we can't get on! That is why black people could never strive in this world, I tell you! I ain't smoking at all, not even a Jamaica cigarette. Anybody have the time?'

'What you want the time for?' Poor ask. 'You have some place to go?'

'I want the time and the date. I going to mark it down.'

But the boys turn their backs on Gallows and went on

talking as if he not there. By and by Gallows drift off, muttering to himself about the evils of the he black race. He went away with a automatic hunch in his shoulders, and his head bend down from the habit of looking for the fiver. Gallows look like one of them fellars with a geeger counter when they looking for uranium: but he would of been satisfy just to find the fiver.

A few minutes later Nobby and Alfy and Syl push off and leave Harry with Poor.

Poor say, 'What's on your mind, you look worried. You want to go up to town with me?'

'I ain't feel like going to town, man.'

Harry was looking as if he shipwreck, and Poor try to cheer him up. He say, 'I know is Jean you bothering about. Don't mind she, man, it have bags of other things in London. You want me to put you on to a little English bird?'

'No Jean might find out.'

'You have it bad, boy. I don't like to see you looking so low. I have some chargers here, you want to try one?'

'It have trouble in that,' Harry say.

'What trouble?' Poor coax. Poor always anxious to get company to smoke weed. 'Come and go across by the park and you could try one.'

Poor push Harry along. Harry didn't really want to go, he just wanted to walk around and mope about Jean, but Poor hold on to his elbow and pushing. They get out of the crowds and went in the park. Poor take out a brown packet and give Harry a cigarette.

'Go on man, light it, it won't bite you.'

'Supposing I feel sick?'

'A old Jamaican test like you won't feel sick,' Poor say, and give him a light. 'Let we go and sit under that tree.'

They went and sit down. After a few puffs Harry lay down on the grass and look up at the sky.

'You feeling hearts, eh?' Poor watching him. 'As if the world is a football and you could kick it all about?'

Every time Harry draw on the weed, as if he taking in something that making him swell from head to toe. As if he raise off the ground and floating in the air!

Worries drop from him like water off a duck back. He wish he had his banjo with him—some sharp tunes and words flashing in the old brain. As for Jean, it didn't matter so much now: if she was here with him he sure he would of been able to make a conquest.

'Poor,' Harry say, dreaming, 'is which part Jean working at all?'

'I tell you what,' Poor say, 'if you come up to town with me this evening we pass round by Hyde Park, and I will show you the place.'

'We will see she?'

'Sure.'

'To talk to?'

'Yes man.'

'You know how these English bosses is, they don't like it to visit anybody when they working.'

'Jean boss wouldn't mind, I could tell you that!'

Poor himself was on his third charger; being as he was so accustom to it he had was to have about two or three before he could get any kicks. And he was just getting on top of a high kick when he look down by the park entrance and see two Englishers come in. Poor had a feeling he see these two fellars before, and he puzzling to remember. Then as they come nearer he realise is two fellars who been following him around for a couple of days.

A fright take Poor. Supposing them fellars was coppers! Supposing they was keeping a watch on him all the time, and come to nab him in the park!

Poor scramble up quick. 'Harry,' he say, 'keep these

cigarettes for me, I just remember something, I go meet you later and collect them.'

'What happen?' Harry ask, though he ain't particular.

Poor throw the brown packet on Harry chest. Harry lower his eyes looking at it.

'Shit man, hide it!' Poor say, and he push the packet in Harry pocket and take off like a bullet.

The two Englishers start to walk faster, watching Poor. As they pass by they look at Harry. One of them start to come towards him, but the other one say, 'Not him, let's get after the other bloke.'

Harry prop himself up on a elbow, wondering if Poor playing whoop with the Englishers.

*   *   *

A lot of things happen that night in Londontown. But to come to them gradually, we start up with Jean. Jean sitting before the mirror in she room, putting on a pair of nylons what have butterflies embrodiered near the heels. She stretch out her legs like how you see them film stars doing when they putting on stockings. Is a funny thing, you might have your own way of doing something, but if you see people doing it another way, especially in films, you think that must be the better way. Before that Jean uses to stand up near the bed and hoist one foot after the other on top of it to put on her stockings.

Inside of Jean wardrobe had all kinds of dresses and shoes what she make off of hustling. When Matilda first come to London she bring dress for Jean what her grandmother send. But Jean only laugh when she see it, and say that she have to get another wardrobe to keep all the things she have.

Matilda there with her as she dressing. Matilda thinking about how Jean making so much money, while she herself have a hard work at a Lyons corner house washing dishes and plates and pots. This was a thought she had all the time, and it was like a battle going on in her mind day after day, because when you come to think of it, what is the qualifications of a hustler? As long as you have a split between your legs you are well away. You don't have to know geography and arithmetic and algebra.

But Matilda come from a religious family. The religion ain't have no name, but Matilda mother uses to go out every night in Port of Spain and stand up by the corner with a candle and a bell and a hymn book, and warn people about their sins. From the time Matilda small she holding on to her mother and going to these meetings, and she have a good idea of the fires of Hell and the tortures and sufferings of all sinners. When she get big and her backside broaden out and her tits get high, her mother warn her to strap everything down and don't cause any temptation. 'Pray every day for the waters of the Lord to wash you clean,' her mother say. 'Don't twist your bottom when you walking, and don't hold up your breasts like you offering them for sale, like them other girls in this neighbourhood.' Jean did tell she that over here in London nobody does mind your business, you could do what you like. But though Matilda make plenty strokes already, when it come to going out on the streets looking for fares, she draw the line. Some of the girls back home uses to show she bracelets and new clothes and shoes—just like how Jean have in her wardrobe. But Matilda uses to say she wouldn't go out on the road for anything. Like how a multiple-sinner would hold on to one virtue and extol its merits, so Matilda feel that if she didn't whore the waters would wash her clean.

All the same, it was a big temptation in London, especially as she was living with Jean.

'You never think of marrieding and settling down?' she ask Jean suddenly.

Jean laugh. 'One of these good days.'

'I think Harry Banjo want to married you.'

'Harry Banjo!' Jean say. 'Harry ain't have a cent to his name. Only dreams. All them boys is dreamers. Look how they talk about buying a house. Is almost a month now and they ain't save up one ha'penny. Unless they give it to Battersby to give me and he spend it. Renegades and reprobates, the whole set of them.'

But still, as she powdering her face, Jean looking at herself in the mirror and wondering if it wasn't time to retire before she get too old and can't find a man. Hustling for fares wasn't as easy as people think, especially in the winter when you out in the open with the wind slicing you in half. Last year she nearly dead with newmonia laying down in the cold grass, and she make up her mind that this summer she going to put in some extra hours so she could take it easy when winter come.

'You don't like Harry?' Matilda ask. 'He look like the best of the lot to me.'

'I don't like fellars who so innocent, man,' Jean say. 'He don't make me feel at home.'

'I would like to married a white man myself,' Matilda say. 'Black man too bad.'

'All of them after the same thing,' Jean say. 'Anyway, I will see you later.'

Jean left Matilda looking at a magazine, and went downstairs to wake up Bat on her way out.

'Bat, Bat, wake up.' She shake him hard. 'Time to go to work.'

Bat grunt and roll over.

'Come on, get up.' She haul the blankets off him. Battersby start to curse as he sit up and rub his eyes.

'Put the kettle on for me,' he ask Jean.

'Put it on yourself,' Jean say as she go out. 'I late for work already.'

*   *   *

When she left him Bat sit in the bed looking at the kettle, as if he wish he could command it to get up and get full and put on the gas and boil. He wish Harry was home: he uses to make Harry do a lot of things for him, and Harry would of make tea. He know Harry was after Jean and he say to him, 'Leave everything to me, I will fix up for you.' From that time, anything he ask Harry to do, Harry doing it, hoping that Bat would put in a good word for him. Bat get to thinking that maybe Harry was a geni in disguise: at least, life wasn't as hard as before. Because for one thing, though Harry ain't know it, he paying all the rent for the basement room, and buying rations too besides.

Bat yawn and stretch and light a cigarette. As he do that he smile to himself, wondering how many of the boys must be lighting up same time? Bat get big kick from the idea of the house, and he already collect twenty-nine quid. Twenty-nine quid! Who would of dream that just by talking about a idea men would give you money? Bat begin to get delirious from the time the money start to come in. He can't even remember who give how much, all he know is that he is the man in possession of the money, and he begin to spend wild. Thinking about it now, he wonder how much remain? He lift himself up and feel under the mattress. For a minute he panic as how Gallows panic when he lost his fiver, because his hand ain't encountering no joy. His fingers scramble about on the springs, and he feel a note and pull it out. It was ten shillings.

Bat jump off the bed and pull the mattress right off. No more money, the ten shillings was all that remain!

Which part all that money gone? Bat wondered. Somebody thief it? I hide it somewhere else?

And then as he cool down, he realise he must of spent it.
No use bothering about it, he would have to make another
collection. Was about time the boys come up with some
more if they really intend to get a house. What would happen on the day of reckoning when the fellars find out that
he spend all their money was something that Bat wasn't
worried about. He would have to think of some scheme. If
things come to the worst he could always say somebody
thief the money. Bat imagine himself telling them: 'Oh
God! You know what happen? Somebody break open the
room and thief my money!' On top of that he would have
to say they thief clothes and wristwatch too, to make it
sound real.

'Battersby, you get up yet?' He hear Matilda voice outside the door.

Bat put the mattress back on the bed and jump back
under the blankets.

'I just get up Mat,' he say. 'Come in.'

Matilda come in. 'As you here, put the kettle on and
make some tea like a good girl,' Bat say.

'You think I is your servant or something?'

'Go on Mat,' Bat coax. 'What you come down for? Like
you know I was thinking about you.'

Bat shift up on the bed and patting a place for Matilda
to sit down on the edge, but she still stand.

'I just wanted to see you before you go to work,' she say.
'They don't have excursion in London?'

The question so sudden that Bat say, 'Excursion?'

'Yes man, like back home to go by the seaside and so on.'

'Oh, excursion!' he say, as if Matilda did say something
else. 'Sure they have. Especially now as summer coming.
You don't see them coaches all the time?'

'I was thinking why we don't give a excursion to Hamdon Court or one of those places, and make money for the house.'

Bat look at the Aladdin lamps on the wallpaper. Jesus Christ! As if the thing really working in truth! No geni actually appearing on the scene, but the way things was working out, as if some good spirit keeping an eye on the old Bat! Look how Matilda come up with this new idea, what could make him make some money. Not only that, but look at Matilda herself in the room, a hefty piece of arse.

'Mat,' Bat say, 'come and sit close and tell me about this plan. It sound great.'

Matilda scotch on the edge of the bed. 'You not going to work?' she ask.

'I don't have to.' Bat done forget work clean, and studying to make a stroke with Mat. 'You know, these days you looking nicer and nicer, like the English weather agree with you.'

'Go on, you only fast!'

But all the same, she getting excited. 'You best hads know that I have a English boy friend.'

'Naturally,' Bat say. 'A girl like you, I mean, you have them wild, eh?'

'You too full of guile! You well know how to sweeten up the girls!'

While all this preliminary going on, Bat hands making some sally across Matilda legs, and she putting up some show of warding him off.

'Don't try that with me—you think I don't know how much white girls you have about the place?'

'Ah, that is only pastime,' Bat say, 'a man must have a little amusement. But you think I really like any one of them? You think I would ever married a white girl? Man, I want somebody who could cook a good pigfoot and rice, and wash my clothes, and scratch my head, and look after me good. Somebody like you, Mat.'

By this time Bat hands have the wanderlust too bad and Matilda shivering. 'Let we talk about the excursion,' she say. 'You could charge about a pound each, and let everybody smoke and drink, that will encourage the boys. Work it out. How much passenger does fit in a coach?'

'I don't know man about fifty or so don't bother with that now.'

Bat couldn't help thinking, in the midst of the stroke, how things was coming his way. And as he wrestling with Matilda, he look at the Aladdin lamps on the wall and he shout out: 'Geni, you are great!'

Was only afterwards when she calm down that Matilda ask him: 'Why the hell you call Jeanie name just now?'

*   *   *

Gallows was going up the Bayswater Road that same night. The kind of thing they use for the pavements there, in the night you does see sparkles and glitters, and Gallows was wondering if in truth the streets of London pave with gold. Supposing one of them sparkle turn out to be a diamond or a real pearl! Plenty time already he find brooch and rings, but all of them was Woolworth and ain't worth a damn. Nonetheless, there is nothing like the hopes and dreams of man, and Gallows was sure that like how every dog has his day, so a time would come when he would be laughing. Like what Alfonso tell him happen to him one day. The tale sound so tall that Gallows had was to believe it. Alfonso say that one day, in broad daylight, he was walking down the road and just by a cafe he see a trail of pound notes on the pavement. The whole world in motion, people walking up and down, crossing over from the tube station by the zebra, standing up by the bus-stop, traffic

going to and fro, and just there, on the pavement, Alfonso
see this trail of pounds, like a millionaire was playing
paper-chase with some spare cash. Alfy say the first thing
that come to his mind was to take a photo. But a bird in
hand was worth more than anything else. Because on top
of everything, people as if they not seeing this money, as if
they fraid to bend down and pick up a note. Well Alfy say
he look around and as nobody want to strain their backs,
he start to pick up the money. He say he pick up eighteen
pounds, scooping them up like if he cleaning the pavement. And nobody bothering with him. In fact, a old lady
bend down and pick up one and hand him saying, 'You're
careless, ain't you?' and another Englisher say, 'You want
to be more careful with your lolly, mate.' All of them
believe that the money belong to Alfy in truth, and this
time Alfy done planning that if a copper only come up, he
would say he was collecting the notes to take to the nearest
police station. But such is life, that nobody make a move to
stop Alfy, and when he finish collecting the manna he duck
around the corner and take off like he on Ascot racecourse.
'And you mean to say nobody ask you anything?' Gallows
did ask him. 'If I lie I die,' Alfy did say.

Gallows never forget that tale. One day he might find a
wallet—he wouldn't have to bend down and pick up
money scatter all about. And in that wallet he would find
so much that his head would spin.

As he reach up by where the hustlers does be spaced off
waiting for customers, he glancing up now and then to see if
he could spot Jean. (Of course, since the law take the girls
off the streets you don't see so many again, but the time I
talking about they used to be spread out from the Gate to
the Arch, and all up Park Lane too.)

Jean was with a English hustler smoking. They throwing
back their heads and blowing the smoke high up in the air.

'What you know, Jean?' Gallows say, but he had his eye on the English thing, a blowsy piece what remind him of the days of the Scandinavian.

'Take it easy Gallows,' Jean say.

'Who is your friend?' Gallows ask.

'One you can't afford,' Jean say.

Gallows nod sadly. 'Is true. I could do with a cuppa, Jean.'

Jean open her purse and give Gallows two and six. Gallows eye open big.

'Like you having a good night,' he say.

'Easy come easy go,' Jean say.

'You ain't seen Harry around?' Gallows pocket the half-crown. 'I looking for him because he might get in big trouble.'

'What trouble?'

'Well, he and Poor was smoking weed, and the police was after Poor, and Poor give Harry the weed to keep for him and out off. I was watching them all the time since they leave the market, and I see everything.'

Gallows was looking hard at Jean, to see how she take the news, because such observations does help him to be in the know so he could talk people business.

But Jean was eyeing a customer who was coming up the road, and she pretend she ain't concerned. The customer wink and she went across to him and the two of them went in the park looking for a handy patch of grass or a big tree.

When she come back Gallows was gone. The English hustler ask her: 'How much you get off him, Jean?'

'I only get ten bob. But he fire off as soon as we get behind the tree.'

The two of them was just lighting up cigarettes when the Englisher say, 'Oh Christ, there's another of those Legion of Mary sisters,' and she walk down the road fast and left Jean.

The sister say to Jean, 'Excuse me, but what part of the world do you come from?'

'The jungle,' Jean say, blowing smoke in her face. 'It ain't no use, lady, it really ain't no use. You only wasting your time.'

The Mary say, 'But this kind of life, my child, selling your body for gain! Can't you get other employment? We have an organisation that will guarantee you a job if you leave the streets.'

'Lady, you hindering my traffic. Go and talk to them other white girls up the road, and save their souls.'

'My child, you do not understand. I want to save you from a life of sin and corruption—'

Jean walk off to meet her friend. Behind her, the sister say sadly, 'We have to put up with so much. You offer people salvation and they laugh at you.' And she went away shaking her head from side to side.

'Christ, these women,' Jean tell her friend, 'they never let you alone. You know what happen the other night? A man approach one of them and ask for a short time!'

The Englisher rock with laughing. 'And what happen?'

'She say, "How dare you, do you know who I am?" I went with him after, all he wanted was a wank.'

*　*　*

Harry Banjo likewise float up to town that night. He didn't even know or care how he reach. It was just as if he wish he was in town, and the kicks he was getting from the weed throw him in Piccadilly Circus. Could be no better place for an aspiring calypsonian like Harry. He cruise around by the theatres, taking down all the displays and putting up new ones: LATEST SENSATION FROM JAMAICA, HARRY BANJO THE IMMIGRANT CALYPSONIAN. And he

putting up some big photos with his face, and some with
him strumming the banjo, and one or two what have him
up near the mike singing. Also, his name up in lights,
winking on and off. This was the place where he belong, in
show business. That is what the tourist tell him in Mon-
tego Bay. Harry uses to play in a hotel there, and one night
this tourist tell him: 'You ought to go to London and
make your name.' And Harry take up himself and come to
London.

You see, though the newspaper and the radio tell you
that people in the West Indies desperate for jobs and that is
why they come to Britain, you mustn't believe that that is
the case with all of them. I mean, some fellars just pick up
themselves and come with the spirit of adventure, expecting the worst but hoping for the best. Some others just
bored and decide to come and see what the old Brit'n
look like.

Every now and then Harry get a break to sing in some
club or at some party, but he was always dreaming of the
big times. And on top of the normal dreams, the weed
have him charge up so much that he feel like breaking into
one of them theatres and going on the stage and singing!

By and by he drift up to Oxford Circus and then to Marble Arch. As if his footsteps lead him straight to Jean,
smoking on the pavement.

'Jean,' Harry say, 'what you doing here?'

'I get a break for tea,' Jean say, laughing.

'You waiting to catch a bus or something?' And then as
he see other hustlers standing around, Harry realise what
Jean was doing. 'Man Jean,' he say 'you mean to tell me a
nice thing like you hustling fares? Is that what you do in
truth?'

'Oh Christ,' Jean say. 'First the Legion of Mary and then
Harry Banjo. You on the reformation committee too?'

'I will married you Jean, you don't have to do this kind of thing.'

Now though Jean was a tough customer, she ain't as hard as rock, and as Harry say that she realise that he really mean it. Jean did know a lot of fellars but none of them ever wanted to married. The nearest she ever come to it was one time in Trinidad when she fall pregnant, but she wasn't sure who was the father and had was to throw away the child. It didn't look as if Harry only wanted to make a stroke and pull out.

'Harry,' she say, 'when you have a lot of money we could talk about that. But right now I know you ain't have a cent.'

'Who say so?' Harry ask. 'And too besides, ain't we going to buy a house? We will have our own place to live.'

'That is only a lark,' Jean say, 'you think them fellars really serious? I know Battersby, he is my own brother, and I could tell you that up to now he ain't give me a ha'penny to save up. If I was you I think twice about that scheme.'

'I buy house myself if my agent sell that recording.'

'Everything is 'if.' If this and if that. You fellars does live in a dream world.' Then she remember what Gallows tell her. 'Listen, Poor give you any weed to keep? You better get rid of it before you get in trouble.'

But while Jean talking she have her eye on a car that coming down the road slowly, as if the driver is a kind-hearted fellar and he looking for hitch-hikers. When the car draw alongside she went and talk to the driver and then she get in the car. As it drive off she look out the window and shout to Harry, 'Get rid of what Poor give you!'

Harry stand up there feeling miserable and desolate, as if all the kicks gone out of him. He haul out a charger from the brown packet and light up quickly to recover the sensations. And as he haul on the weed, he begin to think that he might stand a chance with Jean after all. As if the fact that she was a hustler, instead of putting him off, make him more in love and want to take she away from this kind of life. The weed had him high and the world was rosy again. All he had to do was get money and he would get Jean. He look at the hustlers. How much a night they make? he wonder. Ten? Fifteen? Maybe more than that. He would have to get in the money in a big way before he could take Jean away. He wonder if his agent having any luck with the recording?

He went in the telephone booth to call and ask him, but the line was busy. When he step out two English fellars gang up on him.

'What happen?' Harry ask.

One of them frisk him and find the brown packet.

'You're coming with us,' the tall one say.

'Where we going?' Harry ask. The weed still have him hazy and he can't understand what happening.

'Down the river,' the other Englisher say maliciously.

'What all you want with me?' Harry start to get frighten. 'What this about? A man can't walk in peace in London. That thing belong to a friend.'

'Come along now, we don't want any trouble.'

This time so, sports gather around to witness the episode. And though in fact they don't like black people, they don't like the police worse. So hear them:

'Leave him alone!'

'What's he done?'

'Just because he's black!'

And Harry, as fright take him, turning to them and saying: 'I just stand up here minding my own business and these fellars come and grab me. That is how you all behave in London?'

'All right, all right,' the detective say. 'Enough of all this. You're coming with us now.'

And with that they start to haul Harry down the road. Suddenly now all the height gone out of Harry. 'I ain't do nothing!' he wail. 'I was just keeping that for a friend!'

Gallows come out of the shadows in the park and watch them taking down Harry. It look as if poor Harry can't walk, as if he cripple, the way how he hanging on.

*   *   *

If to say these fellars did really intend to buy a house by saving up money, you think they would have ever start up with the idea in the spring? Only madmen would of done that. If it was autumn, or even winter, it might sound reasonable. But how you could expect the boys to curb their appetites, and hold the lions back, and take it easy when the skies blue and sun shining and things strolling all over the place in tights and low-neck blouse? When summer break, is as if the hunting season start. Even Gallows, who never had a thing since the no-teeth, hefty Scandinavian wench, decide that he getting rusty and is time to make a stroke. Men gone wild spending money on drinks and taking women for coffee and to the pictures and on sightseeing tours. Some fellars even get vap to gon on the Continent and taking off for Greece and Turkey and Rome, and a gang of fellars in Brixton form a group what gone behind the Iron Curtain, saying they would see what they could pick up in the Red Square!

One evening the housing delegation descend on number 13A to see Battersby. Everybody was there except poor Harry, who was serving time for being in possession of. Old Bat get the wire long before that they coming, run out to a few estate agents and collect some housing lists, and was sitting down at the table looking them over when the boys come.

Fitz was the first to talk. 'All right, everything turn old

mask, and I want that three pounds ten back that I give you. I don't want it later, I don't want it tomorrow, I didn't even want it yesterday. When I want it is now RIGHT NOW.'

Teena did make Fitz memorise that speech word for word before he left home and Fitz say them as soon as he reach before he forget.

As for Sylvester, now that the weather getting sunny he start up this knocking-wood-and-kissing-cross lark, and he tap the table, make the sign of the cross with his two forefingers, and swear that is trouble in town if he don't get his money back.

'What's the matter with you boys?' Bat say, sitting there surrounded by these housing lists, and a notebook as if he taking down notes. 'What's all the excitement about?'

'You know Bat, you know,' Nobby say. 'Don't pretend.'

'We should of never trust you in the first place,' Alfy say. Alfy holding his camera like a weapon to crack Battersby head.

'Give Battersby a chance to explain,' Gallows say. Gallows was trying in desperation to hold things together: this chance might never come to him again as long as he live.

'I don't know what want explaining,' Bat bluff. 'What it is you fellars mourning about?'

'The money we give you for the house,' Nobby say. 'We want it back.'

'Well you fellars really stupid!' Bat shake the lists as if they was cheques.

'If you mean that in the past tense,' Alfy say, 'I agree with you. But we see the light.'

'Listen, what you fellars think, that I thief your money or something?'

'We don't want to go down into details,' Nobby say. 'All we want is we money back. Right?'

'If you don't believe me, perhaps you believe what the house agent say.' Bat pick up a list and begin to read: 'Do not miss this golden opportunity. For only one hundred pounds deposit, you can be the owner of a freehold, semi-detached property in the heart of Notting Hill. Four reception rooms, seven bedrooms, two kitchens, two baths.'

'It have a basement?' Gallows ask.

'Sure it have a basement,' Bat say. 'And listen to this other one: "Coloured clients are the ones we want to cater for. We have a large selection of highly-residential houses in all parts of the country, with deposits as low as £95. Our mortgage facilities will tie everything up nicely for you." You fellars think I been sleeping?' Bat begin to warm up as he see some flicker of doubt on their faces. 'Day after day I been going to the housing agents. I wear out my shoes walking. I even been to see a place up in Cricklewood, but it have dry-rot.'

'How far we from that hundred pound deposit?' Fitz ask.

'We not far,' Bat say. 'If you fellars make a sort of last-minute push, before next winter we move into our own house.'

'The only push I pushing,' Nobby say, 'is to push you for my money. Jean say up to now you ain't give she a cent. How about that? Where you keeping the money? Show me it. Show me pound notes and ten shilling notes and silver, Queen's silver.'

Bat rub his face like in disgust. 'What happen to this man at all? You ain't hear about the excursion?'

'What that have to do with it?' Nobby ask.

'You think it don't cost money to arrange a excursion? You think is like back home where you just get some old bus and carry people to Maracas Bay to bathe in the sea?'

'So what you trying to say?' Alfy ask, though he suspect already.

'What I trying to say is that the money invest,' Bat say. 'The money invest in the excursion to Hamdon Court.'

'Who give you permission to invest my money mister?' Syl ask.

'All monies that come into the pool is for the house,' Bat say. 'In any case, what you making noise for? We going to make a lot of money off the excursion, and afterwards if you all ain't satisfy I give all of you your money back.'

'I don't think you hear what I say, Bat.' Fitz talk carefully, trying himself to remember what he say. 'Now for now. Cash on the nail.'

'I will wait until afterwards for mine,' Gallows say, as if he put in the lion share, and this time he ain't contribute a ha'penny.

'Poor was right not to come in from the beginning,' Nobby say.

'But he should of go to court and talk up for Harry Banjo.' Fitz say.

'Yes,' Syl agree, 'they bust three months in Harry arse, and all because of Poor.'

'That is the thing I trying to tell you fellars,' Bat say, and the old brain racing as a idea come to him. 'I mean, we all feel sorry for Harry. As for me, I can't tell you how much I miss him. That is one Jamaican that by blood take. Well now, who had the idea in the first place? Ain't it was Harry? Well now, poor Harry serving time, and you mean to say we going to let him down? You know what is the first thing he will say? He will say, "You could never trust them Trinidadians, they have no ambition." And he would be right! Look how you fellars behaving, as if I is a criminal or something, when all I do is invest the money to make more. How long you know me, Fitz?'

'About five years,' Fitz say.

'And you Nobby?'

'Ever since I come to Brixton.'

'And you Syl?'

'Donkey years.'

'Well I mean. I don't have to ask Alfy and Gallows. And you all won't trust me? Even until after the excursion?'

Bat haul out a pack of cigarettes. 'Smoke man,' he invite, passing it around, 'we got to relax sometimes. I think I might even have a end left over from a bottle of rum what a friend bring for me from Trinidad.' And he get up and went in the cupboard and bring it out.

'You think you should encourage them?' Gallows ask anxiously.

'Well we almost have enough now,' Bat say.

As if they reluctant to let him off so easy, the boys tackle the end of rum that Bat produce. They was just getting mellow and thinking about a game of rummy when they hear a scratching at the door, and as if a little dog whimpering.

'Jesus Christ Nobby,' Bat say, 'you ain't get rid of that dog yet?'

'Yes,' Nobby say.

'And who is that outside scratching and barking?'

'That is another one.'

'Another one! You get another one?'

'Yes man,' Nobby as if he embarrass, 'and the damn thing following me all about.'

*   *   *

The episode of how Nobby get that dog could pass time before we go on the excursion to Hamdon Court. Nobby was living a few houses from number 13A, and he had a landlady with a bitch what make one set of pups, and she come to Nobby room one morning to give him one.

'Mr de Nobriga,' she say, 'here is a pup for you. I know

how fond you are of Bessy, and I'm sure you'll take good care of it.'

Now Nobby had a habit, every time he see Bessy, he patting her on the head and remarking what a wonderful animal. And he even went so far as to take Bessy for a walk in the park one morning when the landlady was busy, though he make sure none of the boys see him. But the only reason why Nobby getting on like that, is because he want to keep on good terms with her. You know the old saying, Love me, love my dog. And Nobby wasn't any different than all the West Indians in this country what catch their royal arse to get a place to live, and have to keep the landlords and landladies in a friendly mood else they get notice.

Because the truth is Nobby ain't want no dog. Back home in the West Indies it have a kind of dog they does call them pot-hounds, because the only time they around is when a pot on the fire and food cooking. Another kind name hat-rack, because they so thin and cadaverous you could hang a hat on any one of the protruding bones. But them ain't the only canine specimens it have, and you mustn't feel that the people down there don't like animals. The only thing is, Dog is Dog and Man is Man, and never the twain shall meet in them islands as they meet in Brit'n. You give a dog a bone and that is that, and if food left over after Man eat, Dog get it. None of this fancy steak lark, or taking the dog to a shop where they trim it and manicure the nails and put on clothes to keep it warm in winter.

So Nobby shake his head sadly, cogitating for a few seconds, and say, 'Mrs Feltin, if Bessy make that pup, he deserve a real good master who could bring him up like a stalwart.'

'It is a bitch,' Mrs Feltin say.

'That make it worse,' Nobby say. 'I mean, she have to be

brought up like a lady. I can't keep her here in this one room where I have to live.'

'Nonsense,' Mrs Feltin say. 'She can sleep under the stairs in the basement. You always said you wanted a dog.'

That was true. Men does have a way of talking big when they feel it wouldn't have any outcome, and one day Nobby went so far as to say: 'Mrs Feltin, don't forget, wherever I am, the day Bessy have young ones you must give one to me.'

When you talk like that to a Englisher he would give you his last shilling—provided he have enough Lassie and Kit-e-Kat, of course.

Nobby watch the puppy wrap up in a white sheet, and Mrs Feltin holding it like a new-born baby.

'You ain't have a male one?' he ask hopefully.

'No,' the landlady say, 'I have given them all away. Don't you want it?'

Well Nobby know that if he say No, he might as well start to look for another place to live. But he still hedging.

'How about if you keep it for me, Mrs Feltin, and give me when it get big?'

'It's big enough now,' Mrs Feltin say, 'and besides, it won't know you for its master then.'

'Yes, I didn't think about that.' Nobby brain ticking like a clock for excuses. 'But how about feeding and so on?'

'Oh, just a little piece of steak, I'm sure she hasn't a big appetite yet.'

Nobby wince when he hear that: stewing meat is the highest he ever aspire to treat himself with, except for an occasional boiler on a Sunday. Then he had to say quickly, as he notice the suspicion on Mrs Feltin face: 'All right, thank you very much.'

And he take the pup from her and close the door.

'Look what hell I put myself in for,' he say to himself.

'What to do now? Give it away? Take a ride on the under-ground and leave it by High Barnet or Roding Valley or one of them places with strange sounding names?'

In the end he had was to put some milk in a saucer and leave it in the corner for the puppy before going to work.

As luck would have it, that same evening the boys drop around for some cards, and when they see the pup they start to give Nobby hell.

'You keeping a managery now, old man?'

'You could train it for the tracks boy, and make a lot of money.'

'What you going to call it?'

'I ain't keeping it long enough to give it a name,' Nobby say. 'Anybody want it?'

This time so the puppy looking at all of them as if they is criminals, and it only going by the door and sniffing as if it want to get away from this evil company.

'Why you don't dump it in the Serpentine?' Bat say.

'Or send it for vivisection and get a few bob,' Alfy say.

'You fellars too malicious,' Nobby say, though in truth all them is ideas that going through his mind, only he don't want to do anything too drastic.

'You really want to get rid of it?' Syl say. 'Put it in a paper bag and give me when I going, and I go dump it somewhere far from here.'

Nobby do that, and Syl take the puppy away and leave it quite down by Croydon.

Seven o'clock next morning, when Nobby turning to catch a last fifteen minutes sleep before getting up to dress for work, he hear a yelping and a scratching at the door. When he go, he see the puppy.

Nobby haul it inside and put some bread and milk in a saucer, wondering about ways and means of getting rid of the dog.

When he was leaving the house to go to work he meet Mrs Feltin. 'Good morning,' she say, 'how is the puppy? What do you call her?'

'Am—er—Flossie,' Nobby say.

'That's a nice name.' Mrs Feltin approve. 'If you leave the money with me, I could get some nice steak for her lunch while you're at work.'

Nobby had to fork out three shillings and sixpence for steak for Flossie, and later had to buy a piece of neck-of-lamb for his own dinner.

Well, the day he get the puppy was a Monday, and the whole week look like it going by, and Nobby low in pocket buying steak for Flossie, and he getting tired of looking after the dog.

On the Friday, he was moaning at work about the situation when an English 'mate' say: 'My missus is looking for a bitch. I'll take Flossie off you.'

Now that a solution was at hand Nobby start to do some rapid cogitation. 'That bitch is from good stock,' he say. 'The mother is pure Alsatian and the father is a full-blooded fox terrier. I wasn't thinking so much of giving away as selling.'

'Give you ten bob,' the Englisher say.

'What about a pound?' Nobby say, and add, as he see the fellar was about to agree, 'or a guinea. Make it a guinea and call it a deal.'

'That's a lot of money,' the Englisher say.

'Think of the dog you getting,' Nobby say.

'All right,' the Englisher say, 'I'll come with you after work and get it.'

Nobby make the fellar wait by the station in the evening, and he went home to collect Flossie. But as luck would have it, just as he was going out, who he should meet but Mrs Feltin!

'Where are you taking Flossie?' she ask.

'To the vet,' Nobby say, thinking fast. 'It look as if she ailing, and I want to make sure it is nothing serious.'

'Quite right,' Mrs Feltin say.

Nobby hurry to the station, and hand Flossie over to the fellar.

'Looks like a mongrel to me,' the Englisher observe.

'No, it is a little Hennessy,' Nobby say.

'Ten bob,' the Englisher say.

'All right,' Nobby say, 'you have a real bargain there.' If the Englisher did say two and six he would of agreed.

The fellar give Nobby ten bob and went away with Flossie.

Nobby went in the pub for a pint of beer and to figure out what to tell Mrs Feltin.

When he get back home, he knock at her door.

'What is it, Mr de Nobridga?' Mrs Feltin say, alarmed by the look on his face.

'Mrs Feltin,' Nobby say, shaking his head like a man in a daze, 'fate has struck me a cruel blow. Something terrible has happen.'

Mrs Feltin held her breath. 'Not Flossie?' she whisper hoarsely.

'Yes. She pass away during the operation at the vet.'

'What was wrong with her?'

'I not so sure. The vet call a big name for the sickness. And I only had she for a few days.'

'What a tragic thing to happen,' Mrs Feltin say, and it look as if she want to cry.

Nobby begin to warm up. 'All my friends admire that little bitch, and she and me was coming good friends. If I had some land in England, I bury her on it myself. I was just thinking how that dog would of gone in the films like another Lassie. Poor Flossie. She gone to rest in the Happy Hunting Ground for sure.'

'Don't take it so hard,' Mrs Feltin say, wiping a tear herself.

'I can't tell you how I feel,' Nobby say, lighting a cigarette quick so the smoke could get in his eyes.

'I wish there was something I could do,' Mrs Feltin say. And then she brighten up a little. 'Wait a minute. There is something. I am getting back one of the pups from my brother—his landlady doesn't like to have animals in the house. You shall have it. No no, it's quite all right, don't thank me. I know an animal lover when I see one.'

* * *

You see, this whole plan to buy a house was doom to turn old mask from the very beginning. Look at all these dreamers, and imagine that characters like these could get serious. I mean, in a way, some of them really have hopes. Harry Banjo dead serious; Fitz, with Teena to jockey him and a fresh picc'n every year, hoping to get a decent place; and Gallows have the idea to occupy him and fill up a big space in his mind. But as for Bat, all he see is a chance to make some money. True, it wasn't frozen capital, but what he bother about? If he had a few quid to spend, he spend it, and hope that by the time reckoning come, something else turn up to keep him coasting, like the way he put the boys off telling them about the excursion. And for Nobby and Syl well, the odd fiver here or there don't matter so much, not that they don't intend to get it back, mark you, from the first suspicious sign, as you see for yourself.

And another thing was the summer. If to say they had let the summer pass and then begin to save, it might have stood a chance, as in the cold months have less temptations. But Bat come up with this scheme a few weeks before the sun start to shine and flowers and things come out to greet the summer. No wonder them boys want their money

back! Because now is the time when fellars have to stretch
their legs and look around for birds, and smoke and drink
and lay down in the sun and enjoy the pleasures of life.

Was no holding back Sylvester in the summer, for one.
He gone mad to see so much woman about the place now
that the curtain of winter coats was raised, and you could
always find him behind some shapely bird. The old sun
only have to break through the grey clouds and then is
trouble in town! And with these new kinds of fabric what
they inventing, some of them so sheer that if you know anything about the refraction of light, you could position yourself in such a way that you take advantage of the sunlight,
and my boy Sylvester would swear that most of the children
he see ain't have a stitch on underneath. Syl was a master of
refractions, like Fitz was a professor of womanology. He
would go up the road and find a good spot. He would
glance up at the sun to see how the rays pitching, if they
sideways or horizontal or vertical, and he might shift a step
or two to get a proper stance of vantage. And as the children coming up the road, one by one Syl would give them
an inspection and a comment, and he have a neck what
could swivel right round without moving his body.

You could say what you like about the old Brit'n, but
when summer come he that have eyes to see let him see. As
the trees take leaf and the blossoms come up from the
earth, so Sylvester shake off the chill and fog of the winter
months, and set forth to amble the streets and feast his
eyes on the contours and curves that proudly display themselves, flouncing backsides and bobbing tits swinging from
left to right, and don't talk about legs.

This occupation is number one priority for Sylvester in
the summer, you can't take his mind off the subject at all.
If you standing with him discussing the plight of the natives

of South Africa, and a chick chance to pass by, right away
you have to start talking to yourself, because Syl ain't with
you at all. Syl out of this world, mesmerised by a tight bottom or a pair of legs. A kind of dreamy look does come in
his eyes, a happy look, a pregnant look, if you know what
I mean. And right away the topic change.

'Oh God old man, you see that thing? You notice the
walk?' And you in for a rhapsody about the women of
London. If the birds know the appreciation that Syl does
give them, I don't doubt a lot might flout the law and
parade in bikinis for his benefit.

This is Syl coming up from the underground: from the
time he left the train, his eyes making a quick scan to look
for something to appreciate, and by the time he get in the
lift he done make a selection. The lift go up, the selection
move off, and right away old Syl bringing up the rear. It
don't matter where the selection going, east, west, north or
south, up the road or down the road. Whatever was Syl's
original destination forgotten long ago, whither thou goest
I will go.

And so, in front, you have this thing in a tight fitting
skirt, so tight she seeing trouble to walk, she have to make
some small steps, and the high heel shoes going clop clop
on the pavement. The bottom outlined in all its magnifi-
cence, contained in the v of the panties. And the movement
of it, the rhythm and flow from right to left, have Syl so
bamboozle that if this woman walking until she drop
dead, you could be sure that Syl going to stumble over the
body. If a fight going on in the street, if people falling
down with some mysterious plague all around him, if a
friend hail out, if a man beating Syl mother to death across
the road—all of that can't detract from the attention Syl
paying to the object in front of him.

More than once it happen that a thing swing a corner and get out of range, and yet Syl keep on walking in a straight line, looking at the mirage in front of him, until he realise that the reality disappear. But that is no worry—it have bags of things going in the opposite direction, and as Syl study the refraction situation, it ain't long before a bouncing pair of tits appear on the horizon.

That is part of the operation—to see, from afar, a likely figure to trail back up the road, and draw quick comparisons with other passing temptations. You could imagine Syl like the lookout man on top the mast of a whaler, with his hand across his forehead to shade his eyes from the sun, and a school of whales appear: 'There she blows! And there, and there, and there!'

To make matters worse, around this time the girls start wearing them sexy cancan petticoats. Syl gone mad.

'You could imagine what you would see if you was a dwarf,' he tell Alfy one day when the two of them was cruising.

'You does only get your kicks eye-gaming,' Alfy tell him.

'Who say so?' Syl say, and he pull out a notebook from his pocket. In the book have the names of a lot of them Continental domestics what come to work in England. Frieda, Maria, Hildegarde, Marcelin, and a set of them, and though Syl ain't fussy about spelling, everyone of them names spell correct, with grave and acute accent to boot. Next to the names he have their off-days, and the hours when he could risk phoning the house where they working.

'Watch at that,' he tell Alfy, slapping the book, 'I have more things than you ever dream of.'

'How you get all of them, boy?' Alfy say.

But Alfy only ask that to crank up the old Syl, because he know how Syl does tackle.

Hear Syl line, when he approach a bird as she window-

shopping in Oxford street: 'Would you like a cur-rey?
Have you ever had a good Indian cur-rey?'

It have men who have some set ideas, and nothing could
change them. Syl pick up this idea that white girls like to
eat curry, and he always with this opening chord whenever
he on the prowl: 'Cur-rey? What about a good Indian cur-
rey?' as if he in some Oriental market offering the spices
and the perfumes of the East.

And every now and then he looking around for a piece
of wood to touch, and pulling out a silver chain what have
a cross on it and kissing it, because this is the time when he
does feel to do that, as if he get excited or something, or
maybe he trying out some kind of obeah that somebody in
the West Indies tell him about.

When Syl stand up in Piccadilly in the summer, you
could see as if he only wishing he could scoop up all them
girls in his arms at one time, so that none shall escape. He
does stand up like a man bewildered, watching a backside
to the left, a pair of tits to the right, a blonde in the front
and a brunette what pass, and as if he wish he had tenta-
cles like a octopus and could just stretch out and haul the
things in, or else tell them to wait so if he don't make a
stroke with one he could fall back on another.

And after all that preamble, you thinking now that Syl
must be like a magnet to the birds. But don't let all that
fool you. Syl was a grand-charger, he was one of them fellars, the way they talk, they make you feel that if a thing
only glance in their direction, another man don't stand a
chance. Like a doctor who could quote all the bones in a
skeleton by some fancy Latin names, and could tell you
about protoplasm and beriberi and what to do if you suf-
fering from any kind of sickness while he himself always
have some evil cough or backache or earache or something, so Syl was.

And the boys hold him down one evening and prove it by Marble Arch. All of them was up there one evening cruising, and as usual Syl start up this talk about woman, and the things he stroke, and how he have to crack fresh eggs in a glass of brandy every morning and drink it to keep up his energy.

Alfy say: 'Wait. Wait a minute Syl. We going to decide this business right now.' And he take a piece of paper and pencil and draw the private organs of a woman.

'What is that, Syl?' Alfy ask him.

Syl look at it and scratch his head. 'Is a horse?' he ask Alfy.

Alfy say no, it ain't a horse.

'Is the Tower of London?' Syl ask Alfy.

Alfy say no, it ain't the Tower of London. 'Think hard,' Alfy say, 'maybe you ain't see one for a long time. Or maybe you never see one in your life before.'

'It remind me of something, but I can't think,' Syl say. 'You know what it is, Nobby?'

Nobby say yes, he know.

Even Gallows had a peep and say that though he ain't had the luck to connect up with one for a good time now, he recognise what it is that Alfy draw.

'Well I don't know what it is,' Syl say in disgust. 'It remind me of something back home. Is a dry coconut?'

'Everybody listen to this man,' Alfy say. 'To hear him talk about woman, you would feel he is a past master, that it ain't have a skirt he ain't lift up already. Syl,' he turn to Syl, and shake his finger at him, 'from now on, the truth is prove. We always suspect you for a talker. Now we know.'

Syl begin to get excited and make the sign of the cross. 'Touch wood,' he say, looking around for a tree or something. 'What it is you draw there?'

'You wouldn't recognise it if it was red, yellow or blue,' Alfy say.

Gallows shake his head. 'You should always look where you going,' he tell Syl.

'I see this man already tackling a thing,' Alfy say, while the others killing themselves with laugh. Hear him,' and he begin to imitate Syl: 'Cur-rey? How would you like a good Indian cur-rey?'

Syl take off growling from the gathering. A few nights later he pick up a Irish thing and bring she round to 13A, where the boys was having a session of rummy. To tell you the truth, it wasn't a bad bird. Excitement so strong in Syl that first thing he knock on the table for luck and make the sign of the cross, and the girl looking at Syl as if she spellbound. It may be she tag along with my boy to find out why he does behave like that. But anyway, Syl making introductions to everybody, as much as if to say, You-all thought I couldn't hold a bird, well look at bird papa tonight!

And Pat smiling at the boys as if butter won't melt in she mouth. Battersby haul Syl to one side and whisper, 'Which part you get that piece of skin, Syl?'

'Just up the road by the market,' Syl say, as if he accustom to picking up things all the time.

'You going to take she for a good Indian currey?' Bat ask.

'I am in a jam, man,' Syl say, 'I ain't have no place to take she. What you think, boy? You think she all right? You think I could sleep with she tonight?' And Syl knock a chair and make the sign.

'You could stay here, man,' Bat say, 'that bed big enough for three of we.'

Syl pull out a bottle of South African sherry what he had in his jacket pocket, but Bat tell him to keep it until the boys thin out.

It didn't look like they would thin out, because while he and Syl talking Gallows and Nobby and Alfy carrying on a big conversation with Pat, asking she which part she come from, and if she like London, and how she hurt her ankle (because she had it bandage), and Pat saying she come from Ireland, that she don't like London, and that she fall off a bicycle and hurt her foot.

'Okay boys, the session finish,' Bat cut in abruptly. 'Mark down who owe who and we go finish off the games tomorrow night.' And he wink at them. Alfy and Nobby take that as a signal to go, that Bat was up to something and didn't want them around to cripple his style. But Gallows remain when the two of them left.

Gallows say, 'Man, all-you have a bottle of sherry there, you think I didn't see?'

'Well you might as well make yourself useful and open it up,' Bat say, knowing how hard it was to get rid of Gallows.

Gallows find glasses and open the bottle of sherry. Syl sit down on the arm of the chair near to Pat, coaxing she to have a drink. He ask she if she playing shy, and she hang her head. All this show of innocence steaming up Bat, and he figuring out a way to make a stroke himself. As for Syl, he restless like a racehorse at the starting line. He getting up and sitting down, walking around the room, knocking anything make of wood, and whenever he get the chance he asking either Bat or Gallows if they think the thing nice, and if she would spend the night with him.

Pat begin to say it getting late and she have to catch the last train up in town, but old Syl telling she to take it easy and relax, and he trying to cuddle she, but she pushing him off.

'If is anything, we could always sleep here,' Syl say.

Pat look round the basement as if she seeing it for the first time. 'I can't sleep here,' she say.

'It have plenty hotels up in town,' Bat say, giving she plenty of rope.

'You think I could get a room, boy?' Syl ask.

'Sure,' Bat say, 'it have plenty in Bayswater, where I uses to live. I come with you.'

By this time the sherry finish because Gallows, seeing the other two fellars monopolising Pat, make himself comfortable with the bottle.

So they left the basement. 'You coming too, Gallows?' Bat ask.

'I might as well keep company,' Gallows say.

'I hope you have your own fare,' Bat say.

Meantime Pat asking Syl: 'What are you going to do?'

'I will get a room, don't worry,' Syl say. It look like my boy want to knock wood bad, and it chance to have some plane trees across the road. Syl run across and knock a trunk and come back rubbing his face and saying Jesus Christ.

'I am not staying in a room together with you,' Pat say.

'What happen to this girl at all?' Syl turn to Bat.

A big argument start up in the road. Pat have she hands folded and she cool as a cucumber, and it look like she make up her mind that whatever happen she ain't going to bed down with my boy for the night. And old Syl like if he in a kind of panic, he turning his back to kiss the cross on the chain and all the time he asking Bat: 'So what you think, so what you think,' like a recurring decimal.

'Let we get up in town first, man,' Bat say, 'and then we will decide.'

They catch a bus and went up to town. When they get down by Bayswater where have all them hotels and boarding places, Gallows suggest that they best hads let Pat go in and ask if they have any room, 'because if Syl go they mightn't give him even if they have.'

'How much hotel is around here?' Syl start to check up on how much money he have.

'This is a posh area, only aristo-cats live here,' Bat say, 'but if you lucky you get one for two guineas.'

Bat was doing all he could to off-put my boy so he himself could try and make a connection with Pat.

'Come on then, Pat, you coming?' Syl hold Pat hand and pull. The two of them went across the road to a hotel, but they stand up by the entrance and arguing. Then Syl breeze in alone.

Bat and Gallows stand on the other side of the road looking.

'That man crazy,' Bat say, 'he can't see the girl don't want to sleep with him? What he believe at all?'

'And Syl wouldn't even know how to sleep with she,' Gallows say, 'it take a hotboy like you, eh?'

'Look how she stand up there alone waiting,' Bat say. 'It look bad. Call she.'

Gallows call with his hand and Pat come back.

'What is he trying to do?' Pat ask, as if she haven't the faintest.

'Well you see,' Bat say, feeling out the situation, 'he gone to get a room for you.'

'And where is he going to sleep?'

'With you.'

'Oh no.' The way she say that, Syl would throw in the sponge if he did hear.

By this time he come flying out from the hotel, muttering Jesus Christ and rubbing his face. Hear him: 'No rooms, man, no rooms. Which part again we could try?'

'It have some other hotels in the next street.'

'Come on then.'

In the next street had a posh-looking hotel, and it had some people going in. Like they just come from theatre or something, with fur coat and bow tie and evening suit.

'Man what you trying to do at all?' Syl ask Bat. 'That place look exclusive.'

'You can't put a decent girl like Pat in any old dump,' Bat say. 'Go on man, they can't bite you.'

Syl would of tried the Savoy that night, he was so thirsty, and anxious to show the boys that he know what he talking about when it come to women.

He went in, but is either they dish him up quick or else he begin to suspect Bat with Pat and didn't want to leave them alone too long, because he come back in a hurry.

After that they start combing all over the Water for a hotel, but as if a hoodoo on old Syl, or else the gods favouring Battersby. Syl only flying in and flying out, and sweating and smoking, and kissing the cross every chance he get, and now and then pulling Bat to one side and saying, 'So what you think, boy? You think she will sleep with me? You think I stand a chance?'

Meanwhile, when they was passing a shop, Gallows break a piece of wood off an old box from a pile of rubbish, and every time Syl dashing in a hotel, Gallows holding the piece of wood out for him to knock for luck.

By this time they reach down by Westbourne Grove and it had a taxi rank there, and Bat tell Syl to try the drivers, that they does know of places. But when Syl went, they must of bused him, because he come back cursing and calling them bastards. He try to cuddle Pat and she turn away.

'I bet I slap you up here tonight!' Syl say. 'I bet I start to get on ignorant!'

Poor Pat just stay quiet.

Bat say, 'Man Syl, you surprise me man. You shouldn't tell the girl a thing like that. You letting me down. You from good family, man.'

'I apologise,' Syl say, kissing the cross. 'Sorry man. But it look like you bring me in a place where I can't get any rooms.'

'You can't say that, look how much hotels you try. But I know three fellars from Barbados living by Tottenham Court-road. They have three bed.'

'You think I could get one?'

'They will give you all three,' Bat say. 'They only have to see Pat and they would clear out and give you the whole place.'

'I am not sleeping with you,' Pat say, 'don't you understand English?'

'Jesus Christ,' Syl say, looking around desperately. Gallows hold out the piece of wood and he knock it. 'I will sleep alone on the floor, and you have the bed to yourself. What happen, you don't trust me?'

'Listen man,' Bat say, getting tired with all this preliminary.

'Let we go up by Paddington station, it have places there, you bound to get one.'

They went up in a side street near to the station where it have some evil-looking joints where Londoners does go late in the night to make a stroke. Some frowsy-looking things going in, as if they just off a beat on the Bayswater-road, and some coming out, and one of them in a red dress scratching she thing and chewing gum.

Another set of big argument start up as they stand opposite a hotel with a neon sign. Pat wouldn't go in with Syl, and all four of them arguing and flinging their hands in the air, and Gallows pushing the wood in Syl face all the time. To make things worse a police car making a rounds and coming up the road.

'Stop leaning on the wall like that, man,' Syl tell Pat. 'You don't see the police coming? You want them to think we is criminals?'

Pat lean off the wall.

Bat decide it was time for some progressive action. He haul Syl to one side. 'Syl,' he say, 'you wait here with Gallows. I will go in with Pat and get the room for you. You don't know how to do these things, man. You getting on so excited you have the girl frighten. Stay here with Gallows and cool off, and leave everything to me.'

'If they wouldn't give me a place you think they would give you?'

'Is not a matter of that,' Bat explain patiently, 'is how you go about it. Look at you, you sweating and kissing the cross and knocking wood like a mad man. If me and Pat go in, I will be diplomatic and fix up for you.'

'All right,' Syl agree.

'The room might be more than two guineas,' Bat say. 'You better give me three to make sure.'

Syl hand Bat the money. Bat went to Pat and say, winking, 'Come with me.'

She went like a lamb with Battersby.

'You see?' Gallows tell Syl. 'That is the way to do it.'

'How she could go so easy with Bat, and she wouldn't come with me?' Syl say. 'You think she prefer Bat to me, boy Gallows?'

'No man!' Gallows say, 'how she could prefer a old hoghead like Battersby in front of you?'

'I would make stroke papa tonight,' Syl say, 'I will tumble she up and down, in front and behind. You-all thought I couldn't pick up anything, eh? You see for yourself? What you have to say now?'

'She really sharp,' Gallows say. 'Here, knock for luck.'

Syl knock. 'She not any ordinary girl, you know. I mean you fellars pick up any bird you could find, and praise the lord, but me, I am selective.'

'Did you give she Indian cur-rey?'

'Yes, you-all could laugh, but I hold plenty birds that way already. I take she to that big Indian restaurant in Piccadilly.'

Gallows yawn. 'It getting late.'

'Yes, why Bat staying so long?'

'I think I going to take a cruise myself,' Gallows say.

'No man, wait here with me until they come,' Syl say.

'What,' Gallows say, 'make you think they coming back?'

'Ha-ha,' Syl say, 'ha-ha. How you mean?' But all the same he start to get suspicious. 'Bat must be only old-talking she for me.'

'I don't know what you going to do,' Gallows say, 'but I cutting out for Marble Arch.' And Gallows walk off, laughing to himself. 'Here, catch,' he say, turning back and throwing the piece of wood for Syl, 'knock and see if anybody answer!'

Syl catch the wood and charge in the hotel. The receptionist was a old fellar wearing a dirty shirt and smoking a cigarette that stick on his underlip.

'What d'you want?'

'I looking for my friend,' Syl say, 'he come in here with a girl. You give him a room?'

'Nobody came here for rooms, mate.'

'Yes, the two of them come in.'

'Well they ain't here.'

'I was standing in the front all the time,' Syl say, getting desperate and kissing the cross, 'and they ain't pass back out.'

The attendant swing a thumb at the back. 'They must have gone out that way.'

Syl hold his head and bawl.

*   *   *

Planning to buy a house is one thing, planning to give excursion to Hamdon Court is another. But Battersby was a old hand at this sort of thing. Back home in Trinidad, nearly every weekend Bat chartering a bus and going round by his friends inviting them to excursion in Mayaro, in Los Iros, in Columbus Bay, in Toco and Blanchisseuse. Being as Trinidadians does thirst after fete as pants the hart for crystal streams, he never used to see trouble to get excursionists.

In Brixton, where the most you could do is cruise in the park or go to the cinema, the news spread like wildfire, and this Sunday morning as the driver park the coach just behind the market by Somerleyton Road, it already had people waiting, as if they fraid they come late and the coach go to Hamdon Court and left them behind.

'Let we have some order man, don't scramble so to get in the bus, it have room for everybody.'

Battersby was standing up near the door with the driver, ticking off the members of the party and collecting money as they get in. It look as if the whole of Brixton was going on this excursion to Hamdon Court. Friend invite friend, cousin invite aunt, uncle invite nephew, niece invite godfather, and so this Sunday morning bright and early all of them congregate in this side street behind the railway station. And the girls in all kind of crinoline and crinolette, can can and cotten, bareback and barebreast, and wearing toeless sandals and with ribbons in their hair, and the boys in some hot shirts and light-coloured trousers what they never get a chance to wear since they come to England.

'Let the old folks go in first,' Battersby say.

Mother, father, uncle and other elders go in, carrying the children. Some of the children getting big cuff and slap as they prancing about with too much excitement. Battersby grudge seeing so much children because they was paying half-price. By the time the old people get in, the others start to scramble for end seat and back seat and front seat. Battersby give up trying to keep order. And the food and drink—well, it look like they setting off for an expedition to the North Pole or something. All kind of big iron pot with pilau and pigfoot and dumpling, to mention a few delicacies, and one old lady have a bunch of water-cress wrap up in a paper, because she say she don't ever miss her watercress with her Sunday lunch.

Some of the boys high already, as if they been feting all night and just come to sleep in the coach. The only time they showing any life is when a bottle of grog passing around.

While all this pandemonium going on, with people for-getting things and saying to hold back the coach while they run home for a cardigan or a thermos flask, what should happen but Mr Poor appear on the scene in a char-a-banc. Whenever a boat-train coming in, especially, you sure to see one of these vehicles park up outside Victo-ria or Waterloo, to convey friends and relatives to their destinations in the land of hope and glory. And fellars who possess such means of transportation don't be afraid to make a few quids. In Victoria one night a fellar from Bir-mingham come down empty, and it look like the people he come to meet didn't turn up, and he start to go around asking if anybody going up to Birmingham, or in transit, five pounds a head? Sure enough by the time he leave Lon-dontown the char-a-banc full up, and he would of made more money if it wasn't for so much luggage the immi-grants bring with them.

Well papa, Poor pull up in this big empty char-a-banc just behind the coach, and announce to everybody that he going to Hamdon Court, and that he was prepare to take a dollar a head!

Hear the classic comment from Charlie Victor, to the English thing he bring with him: 'That is one of the typical reasons why they can't get on.'

Bat wasn't so delicate. 'Poor,' he say, 'pull that char-a-banc out of here otherwise I will mutilate you.'

And Poor, pounding the side of the char-a-banc like if he beating somebody: 'Brit'n is a free country! I could do what I want!'

Charlie Victor tell the thing: 'Of course, legally he could get in trouble plying for hire. I do hope things are settled amicably.'

By this time pandemonium not only existing, it reigning. Some people who in the coach already start to come out, saying they want back their money, they prefer to go with Poor. And Bat have his hands spread out barring them, like how sometimes you see the police holding back a crowd.

'Take it easy,' Bat saying, 'nobody getting their money back.' And turning to Poor: 'Poor, you should be in jail! You send poor Harry Banjo to jail when it should of been you!'

'That is true,' a old woman say, and turn back to sit down in the coach.

But though it had a lot of them who feel that Poor was a traitor, still, a dollar is a dollar anyhow you look at it. Besides, Poor did take the char-a-banc to a garage and get it wash down and polish, and it shining in the morning sun, whereas the coach company, being as how they know it was a spade excursion, perhaps, send a old dent-up coach what look like it barely manage to reach Brixton, and would need a lot of encouragement to start.

Poor instigating: 'Look at that coach! You all not frighten to travel in it? Is so you treating OUR PEOPLE Bat? If it can't start I will give you a push!'

The English driver say, 'Get out of it,' and turn to Bat. 'If everybody's here let's go.'

To tell truth, it look like if everybody really there. The coach full up, and it still had people standing up outside.

'Only one coach coming Mr. Battersby?' a woman ask.

'Yes,' Bat say, 'but there's plenty of standing room inside.'

As things turn out, it had more people than the coach could hold, and Bat couldn't stop them from going with Poor. By the time the char-a-banc full up, Poor ready to pull out first and racing the engine to make style. Bat was just getting in to close the door of the coach when a woman push her head out the window and shout across to the char-a-banc: 'That you there Mavis girl? Come over in the coach, man!'

'I can't!' Mavis shout back, 'we going to start!'

'Hold the coach up,' the woman tell Bat, getting up, 'I thought Mavis wasn't coming again. I want to go with she.' And she went over to the other vehicle.

'All right, all right,' Bat say, slamming the door. 'Hold tight. Let's go.'

Poor take off in front with the engine racing, leaving a set of exhaust smoke behind.

By the time the coach pull out from behind the market, like if fete start up right away. Fellars begin beating bottle and spoon and singing calypso, others beating the woodwork and the upholstery to keep time, people as if they just seeing one another for the first time and finding out that they sitting down far apart and wanting to change seat, some children begin to cry and say that they hungry, three bottles of rum start to make rounds as if they ain't have no owner, as if the Aladdin geni produce them for the excursionists! And man, woman and child knocking back liquor, bottles of pop opening up all over the coach, a woman open up a pot of pilau and start dishing out food, and a man give a little boy ONE clout behind his head and the boy start bawling and crying, 'Ma, man, look Pa hit me!' A banjo and two mouth-organ come in sight, a girl say she feeling hot and threatening to take off she blouse, and a

mother encouraging her child: 'Go on Elouisa! Say that rec-
itation that the English people teach you in school! Go on,
don't play shy' And she turn to her neighbour and say, 'Just
wait, she could really say poultry good, is only shy she playing shy.' The neighbour say, 'Albert not good at poultry, but
if you see him twist! Albert? Where he gone to? ALBERT!'
And Elouisa stand up in the gangway biting her finger and
looking down and swinging from side to side, like how little girls do when they shy, and my boy Albert, as if he sense
a partner, begin to twist in front of she.

And of course, I shouldn't have to tell you that photo
take-outer Alfy is in front of the coach trying to balance
and control his Zeiss and capture the spirit of the moment
on film.

Battersby push his hand out and make contact with a
bottle of rum in the air. He cock his head back and pour
the rum in a stream in his mouth without his lips touching
the bottle. As if his head and his hand catch cramp in that
position, and luckily Nobby haul the bottle away.

'Ah,' Bat say, 'I was longing to wet my throat.'

'Wet your throat!' Nobby repeat. 'I thought you was
bathing!'

'Anyway,' Bat say, wiping his mouth with his hand, 'praise
God we on the way at last. I thought we would never leave
the market-place.'

'You should of bust a crank handle in Poor's head,' Fitz say.

Right down in the back of the bus, Charlie Victor sitting
sedately with the piece of skin what he bring to the excursion. It have a lot of fellars in town who go about as if they
don't want to have anything to do with West Indians. They
talk with their English friends about the waves of immigration, and deplore the conditions immigrants live in, and
say tut-tut when any of the boys get in trouble. As if they

don't want to be known as immigrants themselves, they
talk about coming from the South American continent, or
the Latin countries, and make it quite clear that they themselves like a race apart from the hustlers and dreamers who
come over to Brit'n looking for work. But in truth and in
fact, loneliness does bust these fellars arse. They long for
old-talk with the boys, they long to reminisce and hear the
old dialect, or to go liming in the West End just floating
around looking at the things passing by. Charlie Victor in
Brixton had a way of making it clear that though the gods
will it for him to be one of OUR PEOPLE, he was in a class
by himself. Nothing give Charlie greater kicks than to
stroll through the market during the day and hear all them
housewives call out: 'Morning Mr Victor!' while he nod
and give a little smile. This time so he have his eye on all
them yam and green banana and pig tail and pig foot what
for sale on the stalls, and his mouth watering. If in fact one
of the housewives say: 'Mr Victor, why you don't come
and eat a food next Sunday please God?' nothing would of
please him more. Because the English house what he staying in near the Oval, all he getting there is mash potato
and watery cabbage and some thin slice of meat what you
could see through, and bags of tea—a big tea-brewing
machine like what you see in them cafe always going in the
kitchen. My boy looking thin and poorly and off-colour,
as it were. He get so Anglicised that he even eating a currant bun and drinking a cup of tea for lunch! So though in
fact he fooling himself that he just like any English citizen,
loneliness busting his arse every day. That's why when he
hear about the excursion he grab the chance to mingle
with OUR PEOPLE, to hear the old-talk and to see how in
spite of all the miseries and hardships they could still laugh
skiff-skiff and have a good time. So he pick up this blue-

foot what living in the same house as him, name Maisie, and decide to come.

Hear him as he paying Battersby before going in the coach: 'I heard about your efforts to raise money to buy a house and I must say it is commendable. In fact I thought of patronising the excursion and helping the cause.'

'Every little bit helps,' Bat say, eyeing the thing with Charlie.

'Quite so,' Charlie say. 'Here, have an extra ten bob. And do feel free to call on me for advice at any time. You know I am in the Housing Business.'

'Too many cooks spoil the soup,' Bat say, watching Maisie backside as the skirt tighten as she going in the coach.

Now, sitting down in the back with the thing, Charlie getting in the mood, and his foot keeping time with the calypsoes. When the bottle of rum pass around for the first time, he shake his head, but you could see him watching it like a lost man in a desert who sight a mirage.

'Why ain't you had one?' Maisie say. In point of fact Maisie herself ready to let down her hair, but she waiting for Charlie to make a start.

'They're all putting their mouths to the bottle,' Charlie say disapprovingly.

But when another bottle start up, the temptation was too great. Charlie swipe it in mid-air, and hold it between his legs and make a quick dab with his handkerchief over the neck. It look like he catch the cramp from Battersby: Maisie had was to pull the bottle away from him to get a drink.

'Let me show you how to kill an empty bottle,' Charlie say.

'It isn't empty yet,' Maisie say.

Charlie take care of that and put the bottle upright on

the ground. He light a match and drop it in, and quickly press his hand over the mouth. As the match out and the bottle begin to cloud up, he pull his hand away quick from the bottle and it make a little vhoom! noise.

By the time the coach reach Hamdon Court, you would think the party went out for the day and now coming home to roost in the palace. They finish off three bottle of rum and a crate of beer, and empty bottles rolling all over the floor and clinking. Two pot of peas and rice finish, the children's clothes have chocolate smudge and mineral water stain, and one little girl trip and fall over a pan of stew and splatter it about on all who near. People hiccup-ing and belging, some of the elders dozing. In point of fact, if all of them did get together and went in the park, or if to say the coach did really break down and they couldn't reach, it won't of made any difference.

Nevertheless, as the coach pull up and they see the char-a-banc waiting, as if the party throw in second gear as they dismount, the men making a beeline for the nearest Gents, and the women dittoing for the Ladies.

'Rmember we leaving at six o'clock,' Battersby shout out. 'The coach going to be waiting in the parking area, and if anybody late that is their lookout.'

Meet Fitz and the family as they hop off. The first picc'n, Willemeena, is the one that trip over the pan of stew, and the splattering make a sort of design on her dress, so it don't look too bad. Her hair plait. How Teena manage to do it is a mystery. But it plait, and it have a blue ribbon on each plait. Next come Henry the First. He have a bruise on his knee, and his clothes all dusty—Teena hitting out the dust and at the same time registering some blows for the slow way he coming out. Then Teena herself, all prim up in a cotton frock with sunflowers. She had a hair-do for the occasion and the hair iron out smooth and shiny.

Teena turn to Jean and Matilda, who stand up waiting
for a sort of general dispersal.

'Girl,' she tell them, 'these men! You see how all of them
drunk already? That's what I don't like about OUR PEOPLE.
We not civilise.'

'I for one hardly touch the rum,' Fitz say, grumbling.
'You stick behind me like a leech!'

'Otherwise you just like them!' she say, pointing to the
boys, who was straggling back from the Gents. 'And let me
tell you something, I didn't come down here to look after
the children. You best hads hold on to them. I am going
with Jean and Matilda.'

'Oh God, at least take Willemeena with you,' Fitz beg.

'All right,' Teena concede. 'But you look after Henry,
and don't let me catch you behaving like Gallows and them
other fellars.'

Gallows was sporting a beer right there on the pavement, after taking off the crown cork with his jaw teeth.

Fitz wait until Teena walk off a little way ahead with
Jean and Matilda. Then he give Henry a slap on his bottom and tell him, 'Go on, run after your sister and mother,
and cry and say you want to go with them.'

'Ma say to stay with you.'

'Here.' Fitz give him a shilling. 'That's for you and Willy
to buy lollipop or ice cream or something. Go on, scoot!'

And Fitz begin to look around desperately for a drink or
three or four to catch up with the boys. Alfy haul a flask
from his back pocket and give him.

'Well now,' Poor stroll over as the excursionists going
in twos and threes and sevens, 'what's happening boys?
All you look like if all you mow down about six bottles
already.'

Poor dress to kill, as if he trying to make up in some way
for the treatment he expect. He have on a brown shirt with

black stripes and gold stars, and a sharkskin trousers in light blue, and a pair of two-tone shoes. But all that didn't help, because nobody answer him as they begin to stroll in the grounds of the palace. Sylvester who was keeping his rum in reserve, produce a flask and pass it around as they walking. Everybody had a swig. They skip Poor.

Hear him: 'You all not getting on catholic. What happen, I is a leper or something?'

To see him straggling along, is as if he take the place of Gallows, who was always the one trying hard to buttards. (That's a good word, but you won't find it in the dictionary. It mean like if you out of a game, for instance, and you want to come in, you have to buttards, that is, you pay a small fee and if the other players agree, they allow you to join. It ain't have no word in the English language to mean that, so OUR PEOPLE make it up.)

'What happen Alfy? Nobby? Syl, that is a sharp shirt you wearing boy—you cut it from a sari length? Anybody want a cigarette?' And Poor pull out a pack of twenty and rip off the cellophane as if is an emergency. He pass it over to Syl. Syl take it intact and pass it over to Alfy, Alfy to Nobby, Nobby to Fitz, and so the pack of cigarettes make a rounds with all the boys and escape and reach back to Poor safe and sound.

That incident commemorate the excursion.

'Not even you, Gallows?' Poor ask desperately.

But this time so, old Gallows in glory now that the boys have somebody else to lambast and give tone to. He like a kingpin in the middle of the crowd and only casting some looks of disdain at Poor, and the boys giving him kicks by playing up and treating him as if he win a pools or something.

'All right, all right,' Poor say, and light up one himself. 'Keep to your blasted selves. I have my own rum here.' And he open up a little zipper bag he had with some sandwiches and a bottle of rum. He put the bottle to his head and drink off a quarter without stopping. He cork back the bottle and put it in the bag, and wipe his hand across his mouth.

He did know it was so they would behave. Ever since Harry Banjo went on vacation everybody begin to treat him like if he was a criminal, as if it was his fault. What the arse they expect him to do, they expect him to go to the police and say that the cigarettes don't belong to Harry, that he was just holding them for him? Even Gallows, one day by the market, passing him straight! True he had his head bend down as usual, but still. And Poor pull Gallows up and say, 'What happening Gallows?' And Gallows say, 'I don't want to have anything to do with you, Poor. You send Harry Banjo to jail. Harry was a nice fellar, nicer than you, don't mind he was a Jamaican. The man only in the country a short time and you get him in trouble and save yourself. I low, but you so low you crawling.' Poor pretend he didn't know what the ostracisement was about. 'Oh ho, so that is it! All of you blaming me for what happen to Harry? I must be Harry father! Harry ain't have tongue in he mouth? What you expect me to do?' But Gallows just walk off and leave him. 'A bloody old arse-catcher like you,' Poor call after him. 'The whole set of you is only reformed criminals. Any one of you bastards would of done the same thing.' And when he hear about the excursion, he went and borrow the char-a-banc from a fellar, and only come to try and make ta-la-la and mess up things.

The way he feel now, he wish he did bring a bird with him, at least to keep company. He look around to see if he couldn't spot a thing. Sure enough, birds pelting all about the place in some tight-fitting summer frocks. By and by he

drift away from the boys, hoping he could inveigle a thing
to walk about the grounds with him at least, if he can't
raise a sleeper.

Syl, too, as if he suddenly realise that the palace grounds
is a happy hunting ground stop strolling along suddenly
and begin to swivel his head. Suddenly he kiss the cross on
the chain around his neck and take off, his eyes staring on
some distant object.

'Wait Syl!' Alfy call out, and run after him, being as Syl
was the only one with rum at the moment. Alfy take the
flask from Syl pocket while he was still walking, Syl didn't
even look at him, he just keep his eyes on the horizon lest
he lose sight of his selection in all them bevies.

'Once he start eye-gaming,' Nobby say, 'we ain't going
to see him for a while.'

'The man come all this way to look for women,' Bat say.
'He would strain his eyes one of these good days.'

'We ain't had a drink for a long time,' Gallows say, as
Alfy come back with the flask.

As they stand up to have a drink, they was just by one of
the palace bedroom. You could imagine the old Henry
standing up there by the window in the morning scratching his belly and looking out, after a night at the banqueting board and a tussle in bed with some fair English
damsel. You could imagine the old bastard watching his
chicks as they stroll about the gardens, studying which one
to behead and which one to make a stroke with. If to say
he had all of them there at the same time, you have to wonder how he would call out to them, because he had about
three Catherines, two Annes, one Jane, and a lot of other
small fry on the side. Hear him to Jane: 'Jane, call Catherine for me.' And Jane: 'Which one you want, a, b, or c?'
Or imagine him hailing out himself: 'Catherine!' And

three of them looking up wondering which one he going to send to the Tower for a beheading. And suppose old Henry was still alive and he look out the window and see all these swarthy characters walking about in his gardens!

In reality it was Teena who look out the window, just in time to catch Fitz putting the flask to his head, and she shout out in a loud voice: 'All right Mr Fitz! That is what you all doing, eh? Wait till I catch up with you!'

And when Fitz look up startled he see Teena looking out of King Henry window.

'What you doing up there?' he shout.

'I didn't come to Hamdon Court to drink rum and idle,' Teena say, 'I am teaching the children some history. But you just wait until I get down there!'

Of course I don't have to tell you that by this time all them Englishers looking on as if they never see two people talking in their lives.

And hear Fitz, high with rum: 'Don't teach the children no wicked things! Henry Eight was a evil character living with ten-twelve women!'

'It don't say so in this book,' Teena say, waving a brochure.

'Never mind the book,' Fitz say, 'he uses to behead them one after the other in the Tower. And in truth this palace ain't even belong to him, was a test name Wosley who build it, and give him as a present—'

'Here here, what's all this?' a attendant come up. 'You can't be shouting like that. Move along now.'

And upstairs in the palace, one of the seven hundred servants what used to hustle for Henry tell Teena she best hads don't shout like that through the window, because Anne of Cleves was catching up on some sleep after a heavy night.

We will catch up on some more historical data in a while,

but right now my boy Charlie Victor dying for a drink, wishing he could join the boys, because he know that whatever they doing, is not looking at old armour and furniture and walking from room to room looking at all the paraphanalia that was in vogue in the days of yore. Charlie with the genteel folk admiring the past, but he feeling hungry and thirsty. As for Maisie, she would of prefer to be sky larking with the boys. Funny thing with women, you always feel you want to act as decent as possible, to be on your ps and qs: if people drinking rum and whisky you would get a sherry for she, because that is a lady's drink: if bacchanal and jumping up and revelry going on, you want to keep she aside from all that rough play. And you worrying about the thing, if you should catch a taxi instead of a bus, if you should go to theatre in the West End instead of sporting a coffee in a cafe near the station, if you should take a room in a hotel instead of taking she to some smelly two-be-four room that you sharing with a mate. And all the time, all the woman waiting for is a chance to break away and let her hair down. They want to shake and twist and fire hard liquor, and if you only realise it, they ready to make a stroke at the blink of an eye.

So Maisie trudging along with old Charlie, but all the time she studying that if she was with the boys she would be getting high kicks instead of walking about as if she in the cemetery, because them Englishers, from the time they get in a palace or a tower or a art gallery or any kind of exhibition, they behave as if they on holy ground, and you can't even raise a cough. Another thing is, you wouldn't mind breezing in for a half hour on such occasions, but them places and events, you could spend a day and a night and you wouldn't see half the things.

Charlie start to get restless. 'Let's go and see the gardens,' he suggest. 'It's getting near to lunch, anyway.'

'Come on,' Maisie say, as if she was just waiting for the cue, 'let's find the others.'

*   *   *

On the green banks of old father Thames most of the excursionists was scattered, getting ready for lunch.

'What did you bring?' Charlie ask Maisie.

'Well, I have some cucumber and cheese sandwiches, four currant buns, and a Thermos of tea,' Maisie say.

Charlie groan. All around him pot cover flying off and some heavy yam and sweet potato putting in appearance. Leg of ham, leg of lamb, chicken leg and chicken wing and chicken breast. One woman have a big wooden spoon dishing out peas and rice from the biggest pot Maisie ever seen in her life, except for a few she see in the palace, when they visit the kitchen, and she selling a plate for two and six. A lot of people queuing up with paper plates.

'I think I'll have a plate of that,' Charlie say, throwing decorum to the winds. 'You could have all the sandwiches, and the currant buns, and the Thermos of tea.'

'Come over here with we,' Matilda call them, where the usual gang was sitting. 'We have plenty food, man.'

'Thank you,' Charlie say, and take out his handkerchief to spread for Maisie to sit down.

'Fire two,' Bat say, throwing over a bottle.

All this time the boys attacking chicken legs and some thick slice of beef and ham, and a bottle of pepper sauce passing from hand to hand.

'Nobody ain't bring any curry?' Syl looking around from group to group.

'You best hads tackle a pig foot and say the Lord is good,' Jean tell him.

Everybody sharing what they have with the others, because at times like these the spirit of generosity flow.

'Would anybody like a cup of tea?' Maisie ask, feeling guilty with so much food about the place.

'Go on Henry,' Teena say, 'you and Willy have a cup. And don't spill it. Sit down quiet on the grass and drink it, don't go running all over the place like a blue-arse fly. Fitz, you not to drink any more, rum coming out of your ears.'

'I just had a little to wash down some chicken stew,' Fitz say.

'I know. You been washing down after every mouthful.'

One of the highlights of an excursion is eating out in the open, and Alfy busy with his Zeiss, going around taking a photo at a dollar a time. As he look by the river he spot a fellar rowing a boat.

'Who is that Nobby?' he ask. 'Ain't is Gallows?'

'How it could be Gallows?' Nobby ask.

'We left Gallows in the maze,' Bat say. 'How he get in the river?'

This time Gallows see them and row up close. 'Aye, keep food for me!' he yell.

'Plenty food here,' Jean shout, 'but what you doing in the river?'

'Maybe fish biting,' Matilda say.

'Those bitches left me in the Maze,' Gallows say, coming ashore and handing the boat over to some other excursionists. 'They thought I couldn't get out. I ask as Englisher if he see a party of desperate West Indians anywhere, and he say he see some having a banquet by the river, that it look like if you all slaughter a few animals for the feast. So I say, "Ta mate, if you hungry we will give you a baron of beef." What you have there to eat?'

'Only caveeah and smoke salmon remaining,' Teena say, 'and some patty-the-four-grass.'

'Don't make them kind of joke with me, man,' Gallows

say, helping himself to pots all around, 'I am a creole of the first degree.'

Half an hour later, men lay down on the grass rolling. Some pull out their shirts, some belging, some picking their teeth, and a few old fellars catching a snooze. Bat put his head in Matilda lap and looking up at blue skies. If you ever want to hear old-talk no other time better than one like this when men belly full, four crates of beer and eight bottle of rum finish, and a summer sun blazing in the sky. Out of the blue, old-talk does start up. You couldn't, or shouldn't, differentiate between the voices, because men only talking, throwing in a few words here, butting in there, making a comment, arguing a point, stating a view. Nobody care who listen or who talk. Is as if a fire going, and everybody throwing in a piece of fuel now and then to keep it going. It don't matter what you throw in, as long as the fire keep going— wood, coal, peat, horse-shit, kerosene, gasoline, the lot.

'Boy, we should of gone and see the palace. I mean, that's what we come for.'

'I don't mind visiting the cellars. You think we could broach a cask of rum?'

'Not rum man, wines. Wines and hocks and meads and ports and ciders of various vintages. They used to live high in them days.'

'And don't talk about the food. Beef, mutton, veal, lamb, kid, pork, cony, capon, pig.'

'What about deer?'

'You mean venison. Yes; that too, red and fallow deer, not to mention dishes of sea fish and river fish, and all kinds of salads and vegetables and fruits.'

'Boy, they really used to live high in them days in truth. And pheasants and quail, and suchlike delicacies. They used to kill about twelve cow and ten sheep, and roast them whole.'

'Yes, them was great days, with nights of the round table and Richard with the lion heart and them fellars.'

'Don't forget Robin Hood and the Merry Men. And what about the fellar who was watching a spider and make the cakes burn?'

'And a one-eye test, I think was the Battle of Hastings, when he look up in the air and a arrow fall and chook out his eye.'

'That was William the Conqueror.'

'Nelson had one eye too.'

'That was the Battle of Trafalgar.'

'Boy, I feeling sleepy.'

'Ain't it had a film with Charles Laughton as the king, with a big turkey leg in his hand?'

'Charles Laughton was great. That is actor.'

'You know, old Henry just used to lick stroke, and when he tired, throw them in the Tower and say, "Off with the head!"'

'That remind me, none of we studying poor Harry Banjo. Anybody went to see him?'

'I think Gallows went.'

'How he looking Gallows?'

'He say he will kill Poor when he come out.'

'It would be good if we could get that house before he get out, and give him a pleasant surprise.'

'What house.'

'The house. That remind me, Battersby—'

'Look at that thing in the blue dress. Watch how she sitting down in the boat with she legs cock up, you could see right up.'

'I must say you boys surprise me with your historical knowledge. It's a bit mixed up, I think, but it's English history.'

'We don't know any other kind. That's all they used to teach we in school.'

'That's because OUR PEOPLE ain't have no history. But what I wonder is, when we have, you think they going to learn the children that in the English schools?'

'Who say we ain't have history? What about the Carib Indians and Abercomby and Sir Walter Raleigh?'

'Stop fugging around with that camera Alfy. Relax man, relax. Take it easy and enjoy the summer.'

'Boy I wish I was back home now. You don't wish?'

'Yes boy, life too hard over here, you have to live hand to mouth.'

'I wonder how they does treat you in jail.'

'How you mean treat you? Jail is for criminals.

'Like you.'

'The police evil boy. You read how they exposing them?'

'I feel to piss.'

'Go and find a tree. I just leak against a oak over there.'

'Life funny boy.'

'You telling me.'

'I wonder what o'clock.'

'Syl, why you don't go back to India boy? That is your mother country.'

'Brit'n is my country.'

'Yes Syl, how come you don't wear dhoti and turban?'

'I wonder if I ever get in trouble if the Indian High Commissioner would help me, or if he would send me to the Trinidad office?'

'Man, you don't know if you Indian, negro, white, yellow or blue.'

'All he know is he is.'

'That sound like I dris when I's dri.'

'You see that ad? You see how they fugging up OUR PEOPLE. As if that's the way we speak.'

'Yes, like if you want a nigger for neighbour vote labour.'

'They too evil in this country.'

And so it going on and on, like bees lazily droning in the summer air. It don't matter what the topic is, as long as words floating about, verbs, adjectives, nouns, interjections, paraphrase and paradise, the boys don't care. It like a game, all of them throwing words in the air like a ball, now and then some scandalous laugh making sedate Englishers wonder what the arse them black people talking about, and the boats on the river, every time a boatload pass Syl waving to them, and you could see them white people getting high kicks as they wave back. You could imagine the talk that going on on the boat: 'Look dear, come and see, there's a party of Jamaicans on the bank.' And big excitement on the boat, everybody rushing to the gunnels (is a pity some of them don't break their arse and fall in the Thames) to see. And this time the boys sprawl on the grass, shirt out, socks and shoes off, belts slackened, scratching and yawning and spitting and hawking and breaking wind, and now and then this bacchanal laughter ringing out: some women washing their pots and pans in the river, and the children dashing about like bluearse flies and you hearing the elders shout: 'WILLEMEENA! COME AWAY FROM THERE!' or 'ALBERT! IF YOU FALL IN THAT RIVER TODAY I LEAVE YOU TO DROWN!'

By and by the girls depart for another tour, this time they say they going to see the grapevine that hundreds of years old, and still bearing. Charlie, having the time of his life with the boys, inveigle Maisie to go along with them, and Poor, who was sitting down under a tree all this time by himself, take off after the girls, hoping he could talk with Maisie and raise a stroke for the night.

They didn't leave Hamdon Court until about eight o'clock the night, because you could imagine the confusion, children get lost, a woman remember she left her best pot by the river, two others dash back to buy mementoes, some fellars in a big argument with a attendant because they leave some empty bottles on the grass and he want to know if they can't read where it say KEEP BRITAIN TIDY, one old fellar holding his belly and bawling and saying that he think he have a pennycitis (somebody ask him if he could afford it) and Battersby better get a ambulance for him, Poor discover the two back tyres of the char-a-banc flat and start cussing the boys in general because he don't know which one responsible, and the English driver of the coach threatening to go and leave them all behind and report the matter to the company.

And to crown it all, as they on the way back home eventually, Bat start to pass a hat around for something for the driver. Something for the driver! they ask him, how you mean something for the driver? Yes yes, Bat say, that is the custom, everybody who go on excursions have to sub up to give something for the driver. But he catch them at a bad time, nobody don't want to give a ha'penny, now that the fete finishing they start to find faults with everything, the organisation was bad, they should of had two or three buses, they should of had a guide to conduct them around the palace, somebody lost a wristwatch and the whole coachload of them was thieves.

When they reach back to Brixton, Bat had was to give the driver a bottle of beer what escape destruction.

'Anyway,' Bat say, 'never mind, next time we go make up for it. I thinking of going further afield. These coaches does go to Scotland and Wales?'

'You don't want a coach mate,' the Englisher say maliciously. 'They should put the lot of you on a banana boat and ship you back to Jamaica.'

*   *   *

After one time is another, or every day is not Sunday, as the old folks back home used to say. Some furious cogitation start up, as if the cogitators frighten lest another summer pass and they find themselves marking time left right, left right on the same spot. Still, you don't have to get any bloody airs about OUR PEOPLE, because in this world today they have plenty company. Procrastinators and high dreamers like stupidness all over the place.

And that furious cogitation that was going on—well, is true that it happening among the female of the species, but still, we is we, and after we is weevil!

Matilda make a dash home after work one evening, anxious to see Jean. She was sitting down smoking waiting for Matilda.

'You went?' Mat ask as Jean pour a cup of tea for her.

'Sure,' Jean say, 'when I make up my mind to do something I do it.'

'How he looking? How they treating him?'

'I thinking of getting married,' Jean say. 'I tired and fed-up with getting no place, going on day after day with the same old things and not making any progress. And Mat, even without knowing that I give up hustling he ask me to married!'

'He really love you,' Mat say enviously. 'I wish Bat did care for me like that. So that's why you been home these days! I notice you was looking poorly and I thought you wasn't well.'

'I was thinking,' Jean say. 'Suddenly as if I want to plan for the future and make something of my life before I dead in this grim Brit'n. You think I could have children?'

'Dozens,' Mat say, 'you still young, younger than me.'

'Girl, he was too glad when I tell him. I lie and say I get a job with Lyons, but anyway I will come with you tomorrow and try.'

'I tell them about you already,' Mat say, 'they always taking on people and you sure to get a job. Don't worry about that.'

'I also had a serious chat about the house,' Jean say, 'and you know what? We would try and buy one ourselves if nothing happen with this scheme Bat and the boys have.'

'I can't blame you, girl. You see them on the excursion? All they go out for is a good time. It look to me as if we don't take them in hand, we get no place at all. We just can't leave things to them, they have no thought for the future.'

'I have something save, and if Harry get this job as a singer, we might be able to make the grade. But house or no house, I think I going and get married. That is the thing I wanted to talk to you most about, because well, we will have to live here. You might have to get another place. Unless you live with Bat downstairs.'

Matilda get up on her high horse. 'What you think it is at all? You think I would live with him just like that? We not back home, you know. The only-est way I would stay there is if he married me.'

'Girl, if you could catch him I would be happy,' Jean say. 'That man is a burden to carry, he like a stone around my neck. Since Harry went away, who you think paying the rent for the basement? I don't only pay Harry share but Bat own too.'

'Well look at that scamp! He been coming to me and asking for an ease-up with the rent! He down there now?'

'No, I think he gone to work early for a change.'

'Wait till I see him. Is high time we clear up all this business about house and money and everything.'

'They would only laugh if we talk to them, you know that.'

'But they wouldn't laugh if Teena talk,' Mat say.

And so Jean spark off Matilda, and early next morning she went down in 13A and wake him up and start to chastise him. Bat, waking up from a heavy sleep after a hard night at the factory, hardly listening to what she say. His hands groping for a feel and he have his eyes still close, as if once you do that you shut out the world and nothing could intrude.

'And when we get married I will look after all the business affairs,' Matilda was saying, 'because I know you just can't manage. But I won't tie you down like some people, you would still have a lot of freedom.'

'Come on under the blankets Mat,' Bat say. 'why you so torturous?'

'I hope you been listening to all I was saying.'

'Yes yes, but come under the sheets man.'

'You wait for that. Plenty of time for bed later on, you like a Rush-ian.'

'Come and make one, do-do.'

'No, I got to go to work.'

After Matilda went Bat still lay down on the bed soaking. He was thinking how, even though he wasn't a millionaire, he could be sleeping on top of money. When he roll on the bed he could hear the rustle of notes as they rub up between the mattress and the bedsprings.

The spirit of rebellion take all the females at the same time, or it may be that down in Hamdon Court where so many historical plots hatch they get inspiration. Because Teena take after Fitz too.

'What happening?' she ask him that evening.

'Easy man,' Fitz say.

'I mean what bloody well happening with this house. Also what happening in general, as far as progress is concern. We going to be sitting around on our arses all the time?'

'Bat say he waiting for Harry to come out of jail.'

'I want you to know something, Mr Fitz-Williams. I am tired of all the farting around that's been going around. I want action.'

'Yes Teena.'

'And you know what that mean. You know when I say clear the decks, it is guns away at the crack of the whip. You had a good time this year so far, plenty evenings out to go sporting and idling with your friends.'

'True Teena.'

'Well this year not going to end like all the other years.'

'We having a meeting soon to discuss things.'

'You not going to that meeting Fitz.'

'If you say so, Teena.'

'Because I am going to get things moving myself. I am going to stick pins in your arses, and have the whole set of you as if you training for the Olympics.'

'Just let the summer pass, Teena, and I going to start up overtime again.'

'Too many summers pass, Fitz, and left we standing in the queue. You know when I talking so cool, that is my dangerous mood. Watch out.'

The topic continue in the market one morning when Teena and Jean and Matilda meet up whilst doing their shopping for the weekend.

'You are the treasurer,' Teena say to Jean, 'and you mean up to now Bat ain't give you a cent? What it is at all? What sort of racket going on with our money? I tell you!'

'The excuse that Bat giving everybody is that he waiting for Harry to come out of jail,' Jean say.

'And when Harry coming?'

'Should be late next week.'

'And what going to happen then? He coming back with a million? He coming back with a solution to the problem? Excuse, excuse all the time.'

'Same thing I say,' Matilda chime in. 'If we leave it to these layabouts and vagabonds, day follow day the same way. You is the one to talk, Teena, cause they only laugh at me and Jean.'

'Don't fret your head, I will talk. They meeting tonight, and you and Jean must come back me up.'

* * *

Summer can't last for ever. All them tulips and daffodils and blue skies have their day of bloom and depart. And though you might think that the singsong life the boys lead will go on and on, after one time is another. Is true with them fellars you could never tell what would be the outcome of any conversation. They might say they moving east, and you see them heading west, they might say they coming when they going.

But when the women get together, is a different story altogether. If the boys did know what was going to happen that night, they might of cancelled the meeting. As it is, they come grudgingly, because the summer was waning fast and every sunny evening now meant that things would be grazing about Londontown taking in the sights having a last row on the river, a last saunter on the Embankment, a last roll in green grass under leafy trees. And men who didn't have much luck so far want to catch up with strokes and make the most of every sunny hour. Alfy for one had was to meet a thing by the Locarno in Streatham and wasn't coming, but he meet Nobby on the way and Nobby encourage him to come.

By and by everybody was at 13A except Fitz.

'You see the same thing,' Alfy tell Nobby. 'It look as if Fitz ain't coming. The man right. You know how many birds I could of catch this evening?'

'That's all you can talk about,' Jean say.

'They not interested in any house,' Matilda say.

'What better topic than women?' Syl begin to argue. 'If it wasn't for we men, where would all you women be?'

'As it so happens,' Bat say, 'I have a surprise. I manage to hold back a bottle of Barbados rum from the excursion.'

'Well don't make a speech about it,' Nobby say. 'Haul it out to be destroyed.'

'You see the same thing?' Jean whisper to Matilda, 'I wish Teena would hurry up and come.'

As if Teena hear the door open and she come in.

'Where Fitz?' Bat ask.

'Fitz not coming,' Teena say grimly, 'but I am here.' She nod at the girls. 'You all discuss anything yet?'

'We just going to discuss this bottle,' Bat say.

'We was waiting for Fitz,' Syl say.

'Yes, I know.' Teena went and stand up in the centre of the room. 'You fellars should get jobs as wait-ers. Put away that bottle of rum, Bat.'

The way how Teena say that, Bat push the bottle back in the cupboard before he catch himself. 'What the arse!' he say, and take it back again. As he put it on the table Teena snatch it up and push it under her arm.

'Everybody all right?' she ask. 'Nobody feeling ill or anything? Everybody ready to discuss business?'

'Listen woman,' Bat begin.

'Shut up Bat,' Jean say.

Alfy burst out laughing and Matilda shut him up. A silence descend. Gallows edge over by Matilda and Jean, as if he feel that is the safest place in the room.

'Right,' Teena say. 'Everybody sit down comfortable.' As how you hear them crank up Children's Hour on the BBC. 'Now you Mr Battersby, how much money you have?'

'How much money I have!' Bat repeat. Something was brewing here tonight, he could feel it. He realise he better go carefully. He laugh. 'This woman like she mad,' he say to the room, 'she barge in here and take away my rum, and the next thing she want to know how much money I have! What happen, you want a loan?'

'Go on Bat, answer,' Matilda say. 'You know what she mean. How much money save up so far for the house?'

'I ain't count it yet,' Bat say airily.

'Count it now,' Teena say, 'talk in terms of pounds, shillings and pence.'

Bat start to sing a ditty from schooldays in Trinidad:

> 'Pound shilling and pence
> Good evening ladies and gents
> What I want to tell you
> Is to multiply by twelve twenty and two.'

Strange enough nobody laugh. Gallows wanted to, but when he look around and see how everybody else was tense, and Teena face grim, he changed his mind. Only Bat laugh, but stop halfway and say, 'Like you all plan some trick on me tonight,' and he look at Matilda hard as much as if to say that if that was the case she should of told him. He make another attempt to snatch the bottle from Teena but she back off.

'One of you talk to this woman,' he say.

'Bring the money out Bat, and stop wasting time,' Teena say. 'Bring it from wherever you does hide it, and count it here on the table in front of everybody.'

Bat make another laugh, gill-gill, looking around for support from any quarter. Is a funny thing, but once men get somebody to take in front, they don't mind making a lot of hue and cry in the background. They like to play Follow the Leader: let someone get in the front of the band, and they will follow on making big noise. As they see Teena there now championing the cause, they feeling full of dignity and strength, they beginning to think some strange thoughts, like: Yes, Teena right you know, this lark went on long enough, and: Is time we have a settlement, and even: Poor Teena, she must be feeling it the worse, with two children and they living in a room what even smaller than 13A.

The house might be a lark to them but it mean a lot to Teena. And even Fitz, he wasn't a bad fellar. It all well and good for the boys who free and single to make do with what they have, but what about when people start having family? Them English people don't want to rent from the time they see you, and as for when you have a family!

Bat, making a last attempt to stall, say to Teena: 'What is your interest in this affair, pray?'

'I am representing my husband,' Teena say, 'and the sum of twenty five pounds that he give you so far. I don't know about these other fellars.'

'Go on, count the money Bat,' Alfy say.

'Yes Bat, count it,' Nobby say.

'You might as well,' Syl join the others.

Only Gallows waiting to see which way the wind blow. Gallows did think so much about this house that he frighten lest he damage his chances either way.

'All right, all right,' Bat say. 'What you all think? I thief the money? I have every black cent here.'

'Bring it,' Teena say. 'Bring it here and count it.'

'Raise up off the bloody bed,' Bat tell Jean and Matilda, who was sitting on it. When they get up he yank the mattress aside. Fivers and pound notes and other sterling in paper money lining the spring. They have the indentations and wrinkles from nights of sleep.

'Look it there,' Bat say, 'you satisfy now? I don't know what happen to this woman here tonight, *oui*. Like she gone mad.'

'What about the silver?' Teena ask, 'and the coppers?' And she throw a quote at Bat: '"Little drops of water, little grains of sand, make the mighty ocean, and the beauteous strand."'

'Don't sing no bloody Sunday school hymn for me,' Bat glare at she before he pull out a Ovaltine tin from under the bed. He open it and cant the money out on the mattress. 'I hope all of you satisfy now,' he say. 'I thought I had friends, but all of you worse than English people.'

'Today is the day of reckoning,' Teena say, 'and action. Count it, down to the last cent.'

'Count the blasted thing yourself,' Bat say.

'I will count it for you, Bat,' Gallows say, though to tell the truth if he reach up to twenty he wouldn't know to go any further. But what the scamp had in mind was that maybe his lost fiver among those on the bedspring, and he want to make a search. It suddenly occur to him that he wouldn't even know if it was there, he would have to look at the number on one quickly and tell them that he know it by the number.

But Teena tell him: 'You keep your evil hands off. I understand that you booking basement room in the house and you ain't even contribute a fart.' She turn to Matilda and Jean. 'We will count it.'

To do that she had to let go of the bottle, putting it down on the table, and Bat snatch it up like a seagull swooping on a fish, and off with the cork and gulp some down quick. He make a loud Ah and smack his lips. 'If I had friends I would of offered them a drink,' he say, and he went in a corner hugging the bottle, jamming up against the wall as if the genis on the wallpaper could console him in this hour of stress.

Everybody else crowd round the table as the girls begin to count the money, sorting out fivers from ones and halfcrowns and shillings and pence.

'You know how much money here?' Teena turn to ask Bat.

'I say I ain't count it,' Bat say. 'You don't understand Queen's? You want me to put it in West Indian for you? I have not assessed the sterling situation. Parse and analyse that sentence if you could, you old *macoumere*.'

'How much there Teena, how much?' Gallows seeing so much money he thinking they could buy a mansion up in Hampstead. He make another try to investigate the fivers, but from the time he push his hand she give him ONE lash.

'One hundred and twenty one pounds, eight shillings and fivepence ha'penny,' Teena announce like is a big scene in a TV drama.

'You didn't count the farthings,' Bat say.

Nobby whistle and dig Alfy. 'We holding big, boy!'

And Syl say, 'I didn't know we pass the hundred mark, man.'

'Some of that money is my personal property,' Bat come to the table. 'I better sort out the sheeps from the goats.'

'Don't touch that money Bat!' Teena warn him. 'Leave everything just as it is. Everybody sit back down as they was before. This is only Chapter One.'

The boys find themselves obeying automatically, except for Bat—but at this stage Teena holding the floor.

'All right.' She stand up with arms akimbo. 'Next on the programme is Harry Banjo. We start off by making some of you shame. Anybody ever heard of him? Anybody here friendly with him? Anybody went to see him since he get in trouble? He is your friend, if wasn't for him this idea wouldn't of come up, not that is anything brilliant, but any spark in company like this is a conflagration.'

'I went Teena.' Gallows raising his hand as if he in a class and the teacher ask a question.

'Was you delegated to go or you went on your own?'

'How you mean?'

'You went on your own?'

'Yes, I just breeze in one day as I was passing the jail, I carry a packet of cigarettes for him too, Teena. Twenty.'

'Anybody else went?'

Syl clear his throat. 'Well I went one day, but it wasn't time for visiting hours.'

'Yes. I remember that time,' Nobby say, 'I was with Syl, and the both of we wanted to go.'

Teena turn to the girls. 'You see these liars and renegades. However, I going to keep to the point. Now Mr Battersby, you say you waiting for Harry to come out of jail. What difference that going to make, pray?'

'How you mean what difference?' Bat say. 'It was the man idea. And besides if he sell that recording he will be in big money.'

'Let me tell you something,' Teena say, 'that recording ain't going any place but the dustbin. Who fool Harry that he could sing? Is all right for a little club session or party, but you think Harry ever going to be a Beatle? More likely a weevil.'

'You can't say that,' Jean say, 'he have a good voice, man. He might stand a chance.'

'All right, I give you that,' Teena say. 'But even so, that's his own business, it ain't have nothing to do with the house. Bat talking as if we expect Harry to buy a house for we to live in.'

Bat look at the wallpaper as if he only wishing he could say: 'Geni, come and take this woman away and lose she in the heart of deepest Africa.'

Teena went on: 'So all right. So much for Harry. Chapter Two is this: What you all actually do about this house? You been to see any agents? You been to see any places?'

Everybody look at Bat. Bat say: 'Ask these fellars, or ask Fitz, I show them all the lists the other day. I went to agents all about until I get tired walking.'

Teena wave she hand. 'Anybody could get lists, don't act as if you climb Mount Everest. But you actually discuss the matter with anybody?'

Bat say: 'It have a agent in Croydon who say come back as soon as we raise about two hundred and he will fix up.'

'So far so good. We can't be fussy which part the house is, because we won't have much choice.'

'I won't mind Mayfair or Belgravia—or the Chelsea Embankment at a pinch,' Bat say.

'What about a cottage next to Buckingham Palace?' Teena ask sarcastic. 'Imagine you get up in the morning and standing by your window yawning and stretching, and you wave across the lawn: "Morning neighbour!"'

Everybody had a laugh at this, but to show you how things was reaching a serious stage, Alfy say, 'It shouldn't be too far from where we working, though.'

'That's the first constructive remark any of you make tonight,' Teena say, 'it still have hope of salvation for the lot of you. Okay, we concentrate on the area around here. Next on the programme, we come back to money. Say we have a hundred and twenty, because it hopeless to ask this reprobate to account for all of it. I suppose we should praise God he didn't squander the lot.'

Now all this time Bat was keyed up for when they raise this point. If they only know that the two hundred mark must have been past already! If in the general sweep that Teena was making she wash away his sins, he wouldn't have anything to worry about immediately.

Bat take the turn of the tide in a flash. 'As a matter of fact Teena,' he say, 'I been listening to you all this time, and to tell you the truth so far you talking good sense. You know how hard it is to control these boys, they like little children. But with this inspiring discourse that you giving them, I sure they will try to be better in future.'

Teena glare at Bat. 'I will leave Matilda to settle with you, and hope it not too late to save your soul. Nobby, how much money you working for?'

'I could hit around twenty with overtime.'

'There you are. And I sure you fellars working for around the same. Now you mean to tell me that four hulking men like you can't raise eighty pounds?'

'What about me?' Gallows ask in alarm. 'I will get a work tomorrow please God.'

'And Fitz and Harry?' Bat ask.

'Don't worry about Harry,' Jean say, 'he will give his share.'

'And for Fitz,' Teena say, 'I will show you all how serious I is about this whole matter.'

She open her purse slowly. She take out some weather-beaten notes and some change, and put it down on the table. For the first time it look like she was going to break down, her voice get husky.

'That's ten pounds. We had it put aside to buy some winter clothes for the children.'

Well! You talk about melodrama! Everything what Teena say and do so far was as nothing to this. Fellars start to scratch their heads and look around, Matilda and Jean as if they want to cry, Bat make as if he want to laugh but change his mind, and Gallows suddenly begin to make an earnest search about the room for the elusive fiver, as if he want to find it and plonk it down on the table right away to augment the funds. Then Syl pull out a ten shilling note and put it down on the table without a word. Alfy put something too, glaring at Syl as much as if to say he shouldn't of done that because it put them all in jeopardy. Nobby also come up with his quota.

Hear Bat: 'When I get pay tomorrow I will put in a fiver.'

'You will put in more than a fiver Mr Battersby,' Teena say, 'from what I understand you and Gallows is the only-est ones who ain't contribute to this house. Fair is fair, and you will have to catch up with the others if you want to stay in.'

'Well I glad all of that settle now,' Bat say quickly, 'it really take a load off my mind. Now that things under control we could really do something. For a start let me collect all that money and put it away in a safe place.'

'I don't want nobody sleeping on my money, man,' Syl growl.

'Me too, 'Nobby say.

'Nor me,' Alfy say.

Teena wait until Bat went to the table and stretch out his hand like one of them mechanical shovel you does see on building site. Then she give him ONE lash. 'Keep your digits off. From now on Jean will keep the money.'

While Jean was collecting with Bat looking on like a hungry hawk, Teena continue: 'Last thing on the programme, I want to say a few words.' (Skiff-skiff and gill-gill laughter.) 'Shame, shame and sorrows, is what scalliwags and scoundrels like the set of you bring on the heads of OUR PEOPLE. Everything is a skylark and a fete and a bacchanal. None of you ever get serious; if I didn't take Fitz in hand, he would gamble every night and go sporting and looking for white girls. You all can't even get serious about a thing like housing. You know the distresses we have to go through, you know the arse black people see to get a roof over their heads in this country, and yet, the way you all behave is as if you haven't a worry in the world. No ambition, no push. Just full your belly with rum and food, and you all belge and fart around and look for lime to pass the time, walk about, catch women, stand up by the market place talking a set of shit day in and day out. That is what you come to Brit'n to do? Fellars like you muddy the waters for West Indians who trying to live decent in the country. They should line the lot of you up against a wall and shoot you!'

'Tell them Teena, tell them,' Nobby say as she pause for breath.

'Is no bloody joke,' she say, 'it have a time and place for everything. You fellars only wasting your lives.'

Gallows make the sign of the cross with his forefingers and kiss it. 'Tomorrow self please God I going to look for a work, whatever it is, if is not executing I won't mind directing a bank or something. I will give up the search for that fiver that I lost one day and concentrate on reality.'

'You all should think of marrieding and settling down,' Teena went on ignoring Gallows. 'A good woman will soon straighten out the set of you.'

'I hope you listening well Bat,' Matilda say.

'Nobody ain't going to clip my wings,' Bat say. 'Look what Teena do to Fitz. Look what she trying to do with all of we.'

'At least Fitz have more ambition than you,' Teena say. 'You just wait until Matilda hog you.'

Bat laugh. 'Mat, listen to this woman. Tell she how we going to live a life of harmony, that you going to allow me to do what I want, and come and go as I please.'

'Yes do-do,' Mat say, but she turn to wink at the girls, as much as if to say, 'Just let me get my hands on the rascal and I will have him straight as a pin and steady as a rock.'

Bat begin to feel he could take over command of the situation now. 'Well girl Teena,' he stand up near to her and put his hand on her shoulder, 'I really glad you come here tonight and sweep the clouds away and let us know what the position is. I for one think it was a pep talk that these boys needed, and I hope they listen good. What you say make sense, and I only hope these boys make up their minds to turn over a new leaf.'

Teena shake his hand from her shoulder. 'Don't think you could sweet-talk me, Bat. I know you are the ringleader.'

'Let bygones go by,' Bat say, anxious to get back into

stride. 'We could have a drink now? I mean as a sort of little celebration now that everything settle.'

'Bring the bottle,' Teena say.

Bat went in the corner where he left it and bring it come. Teena pour three glass full. She give Jean and Matilda and keep one for herself.

'You all can have the balance,' she say. This time so the bottle down in short pants.

'Oh God,' Bat say, 'you not only taking over my affairs and want to run my life, but you drinking my rum too!'

The three girls went upstairs to Jean room with their drinks, and the boys start up a discussion on the turn of events. They argue and talk for about a hour, treating the rum gentle to stretch it out, saying what and what they wouldn't do now that they realise they on the wrong path. Gallows asking if they know of any jobs, Nobby saying that when he go back home he will clean out his room first thing because he never done it since he move in. Alfy swear he would take his clothes to the laundry, and Syl say he will look for a good wife and he wouldn't mind if even she white, as long as she could cook a good cur-rey. And all of them giving Bat tone how Teena dominate the scene, but Bat don't care because in his mind he praising the Lord that he get away with all the swindling he was doing.

A little later he produce a pack of cards and all the resolutions disappear as they start up a session of rummy at a tanner a corner.

* * *

Of all living things, Man is the only one who does worry. From the minute he born he have to start hustling for food, clothes and shelter, and he hardly live a few years before he have to begin to worry about death. And in them few years, think of all the contention and bafflement and the

fights and arguments and struggles and hardships and sorrows. So really speaking, if it have fellars who seem to be
breezing through life without a care, you have to say good
luck to them. If a fellar could afford to laugh skiff-skiff at
something what making you cry, how you could blame
him? You wish you could of laugh yourself! It have great
philosophers who wish they was like that, who wish they
haven't to bother with the international situation, what
happening behind the Iron Curtain, what going on in the
Middle East, if it going to be a labouring year or a conser-
vative year in the old Brit'n. And men all over the place
shitting their pants wondering what they would do if they
lose their jobs, they have the mortgage to pay, they have
the rates to pay, they have insurance to pay.

It only had a few days left for Harry Banjo to escape from
jail (when they hold one of the boys and he get out you have
to call it an escape). And yet Bat was sure something bound
to happen. If the worse come to the worse he would go and
put a fiver on a twenty-to-one horse, and ask the geni to
make sure it come in. As things turn out, he didn't have to.
One morning he had a visitor, and an Englisher to boot.

'Good morning,' Bat say, 'What can I do for you?'

'I am looking for Harry Banjo,' the fellar say.

'Harry is on holiday,' Bat say, 'he is visiting the Scottish
side of his family in North Ireland.'

'He never told me that,' the fellar frowned. 'I'm his agent.'

'Oh. Please come in.' Bat widen the door and his mouth.
'Is it about the recording?'

'Yes,' the agent say. 'When is he coming back?'

'In a few days. You have any message for him? I am his
first cousin on the West Indian side.'

'A bit of good news,' the agent say. 'You could tell him to
call me as soon as he gets back.'

'I always know that boy would make good. Calypso is his life. How much money he going to get?'

'I'd rather discuss that with him,' the agent say.

'It's all right. He tell me everything being as I is his first cousin. Fifty? A hundred?'

'Depends on the contract.' The agent get up to go.

'Have a cup of coffee,' Bat say.

'No thanks.' But he stop by the door. 'Did you say you're his cousin?'

'First,' Bat say.

'Maybe you could help me, I need a lot of information. Facts about the banana plantations in Jamaica, his childhood struggles, that sort of thing.' He sigh. 'What I really need is a gimmick to sell him to the English public.'

'A gimmick?'

'Yes, you know, something outstanding and special, tragic or funny. I don't suppose you know of anything?'

'I notice he have a peculiar way of hitting high C, if that's what you mean.'

The agent laugh and had a look at 13A. 'How long has he been here?'

'Oh, this old room is just a temporary measure,' Bat say. 'Actually he renting a pied de terrace in Chelsea. Near the Embankment.'

'H'mm. Pity you didn't know of some angle to arouse public sympathy.'

Bat wish he did encourage Harry Banjo to lose a little finger or a toe. 'Let me call my sister,' he say, because perhaps Harry tell Jean things that nobody else know.

He went by the door and shout out for Jean. When she come he introduce she to the agent and say, 'I tell him that Harry is in Ireland at the moment but we expect him back in a few days. He want to find out a few things.'

'Maybe he could help Harry,' Jean say, 'but *you* won't think of that. Why you don't tell the man the truth?'

'You don't understand,' Bat say quickly, 'it look like they want Harry to sign a contract.'

'That's the part you studying. You don't think about how he in jail for something he never do?'

'What's this about?' the agent ask.

Bat hold his head and groan, and went and sit down on the bed as Jean start to tell the whole story. When she finish Bat fling his hands in the air and say, 'All right, you cripple the man style for always. Now he don't stand a chance in a million years.'

But the agent begin to get excited. 'You mean this chap Poor is the real culprit? Couldn't any of you do anything when it happened?'

'We write the Home Office,' Bat say.

'We didn't write no blasted Home Office,' Jean say. 'Nobody didn't do anything except feel sorry.'

'Well now,' the agent begin to pace about between the table and the fireplace, and Bat watching him anxiously, 'maybe we could work an angle there.' Now as if he talking to himself. 'Yes, it might work . . . Innocent Calypsonian Takes Blame For Friend . . .'

'You got it wrong,' Jean say.

'He ain't got it wrong at all,' Bat say, jumping up. 'That's exactly what happen. Like that character in that book, am, am, what the dickens it is again—'

'A Tale of Two Cities,' the agent say.

'Yes,' Bat say, 'greater love hath no man. I mean, that is the sort of thing you want? I would of told you if I did know.'

'I could exploit the coloured angle,' the agent say.

'Help yourself,' Bat say, 'red white and blue—.'

'He hasn't any relative here?'

'Only me.'

'Well now, thanks a lot.' As if he want to kiss Jean, who stand up like she in a daze with all this. 'I must go and see him personally.'

'Not today,' Bat say. 'He specially ask me to visit him today, being as is his birthday.'

'This is important,' the agent say impatient.

'But this is more important,' Bat say. 'I sorry, but I got to go. I don't want to let him down.'

'Look here—' Jean begin, but Bat cut in loudly. 'Maybe we could arrange something,' he say, stepping in front of Jean, 'we could share the time if they allow it. As long as I see him first.'

'Well, goodbye,' the agent say.

'See you in jail,' Bat say.

As he close the door Bat start to dance about the room like a madman.

'I don't know what happening,' Jean say, 'but if it make you glad I sure is something bad.'

'We got a gimmick, that's what,' Bat say. 'Is a lucky thing Harry went to jail.' He stay still with a thought. 'But I should of ask the agent for a deposit.'

*   *   *

The last rose of summer was fading when Harry Banjo come out of jail, but the rosiness of the future help him to forget the past. The agent went to town on the story, big photo in the papers, and this ballad about the loyalty and bonds of friendship that exist among the coloured members of the community. Poor turned out to be a destitute with a large family to support and that's why Harry Banjo, being single and of chivalrous mettle rarely seen in modern times, decide to take the rap. The story went on that he would be cutting his first disc soon, with some numbers that he compose while awaiting Her Majesty's pleasure in the Brixton jail.

Down in Brixton OUR PEOPLE rise in support. One or
two reporters who went sniffing around get some tall tales
about how Harry do good in the neighbourhood, giving
money to the needy, giving away his clothes to the naked,
visiting the sick, succouring the sorrowful. And as for tal-
ent, his ancestors were kings of calypso in the islands.

As for Poor, the rumour went round that he immigrate
to Bristol, though Gallows say he know for sure that is
Nottingham and not Bristol, but Poor didn't want anybody to know which part he was going.

'Is a good thing anyway,' Harry say, 'otherwise I would
of wash his arse with licks.'

'All's well that ends well,' Bat say. 'If wasn't for Poor you
wouldn't have a gimmick.'

'All the same,' Harry say, 'I would of beat him like a snake.'

'From now on,' Bat say, 'we have to take it easy. You
have to think of your reputation. We are all reformed characters. You have to be trained for stardom and popularity.
You could sign your name?'

'What you take me for?' Harry ask.

'I only thinking of all them autographs you will have to
sign. Another thing, you best hads make me your agent. If
I wasn't a fast thinker, you wouldn't be where you is now.
I can learn the ropes quickly. I will read Stage and Variety
and be your emperor sario.'

'You take it easy, you wouldn't even be my sisio. Where
I going you can't follow.'

'It's better to have one of OUR PEOPLE collecting that ten
per cent commission than any fuggup Nordic.'

'It will make for better relations for me to have a English
agent,' Harry say. 'We got to intergrade if we want to live
in peace and harmony.'

'Anyway,' Bat say, 'what I can be is your righthand man.
You know, somebody who could check them contracts and

keep off the Press and make arrangements for your tours
and appearances, and see that you not disturbed while you
composing.'

'I know who are my friends now,' Harry say.

'What happen, happen for the best. Who look after your
banjo while you was away? You know how many times I
was tempted to flog it, but I say no, that is Harry bread
and butter. And all these weeks you been away, I pay the
rent and keep the room for you.'

'You lie. Was Jean who pay.'

'Talking of Jean remind me of another thing,' Bat say.
'You got to remember I am the only relative, I will have to
give she away in marriage.'

'I don't know how a sweet girl like Jean could have a
brother like you.'

'Just remember we have to keep the business in the family,' Bat say. He went across by the fireplace where piece
of the Aladdin wallpaper did sever relationship with the
wall and was dangling. He tear it off gently and put it in
his pocket.

'What you want that for?' Harry ask. 'A memento?'

'No,' Bat say. 'The girls going to look around for some
things for the new house, and I want Mat to get this paper.'

'You don't want no stupid paper like that, man,' Harry
say. 'We got to have contemporary designs.'

But Bat only smile and look around at the walls. You
could see as if he wishing he could strip the lot and carry it
go in new house.

Ready to find
your next great classic?

Let us help.

Visit prh.com/penguinclassics

PENGUIN
CLASSICS